A Dangerous Liaison

"So, you have never been kissed!" exclaimed the marquis.

"It is not the same in France," said Yvonne primly. "French girls are not so forward as English ones."

She stopped to sniff a rose and he looked down at her, half exasperated, half amused. "Would you like me to kiss you?"

Her eyes met his and then she automatically veiled them with her long eyelashes in a coquettish gesture. "But why?"

Suddenly, the answer flew though the marquis's thoughts: *Because I think I might be a little in love with you*, but aloud he said, "For amusement. Would you not like to have the experience?"

"Perhaps," she said slowly. "For it would not matter. After York, I will not see you again. Yes, perhaps I will try." She turned her face up to his.

He cradled her face in his hands and gently kissed her on the mouth. Such innocence, he thought in a dazed way, such piercing sweetness near to pain. And then a black wave of passion seemed to crash across his brain, and the next thing he knew, she was struggling free of his lips.

"I am so sorry," he said huskily. But she turned and ran away from him, through the flower beds, and out of the gate....

Praise for Marion Chesney's
Travelling Matchmaker Series

EMILY GOES TO EXETER

"A delightful lead-off for Chesney's latest Regency romance series."

—*Booklist*

"Thoroughly delightful reading, Chesney's novels are the best Regency romances since Georgette Heyer."

—Baton Rouge *Advocate*

PENELOPE GOES TO PORTSMOUTH

"An adventure of a lifetime involving deaf-mute servants, death by hanging, kidnapping, and attempted murder! Makes you wish to read the next one in the series."

—*Rendezvous*

"Marion Chesney has a way of snagging the reader's attention in the first chapter. She has done her research in the period, she can create characters and develop a plot, and she can tell a story."

—*Knoxville News-Sentinel*

Yvonne Goes to York

BEING THE SIXTH VOLUME OF
THE TRAVELLING MATCHMAKER

Marion Chesney

ST. MARTIN'S PAPERBACKS

YVONNE GOES TO YORK

Copyright © 1992 by Marion Chesney.

Series border illustrations on cover by Leslie Pellegrino; main illustration on cover by Ralph Amatrudi.

Library of Congress Catalog Card Number: 92-2752

ISBN 0-312-92849-1

Printed in the United States of America

St. Martin's Press hardcover edition/August 1992
St. Martin's Paperbacks edition/December 1992

10 9 8 7 6 5 4 3 2 1

The Travelling Matchmaker
is dedicated to Christine and Colin Timms
with love.

about that letter, the more she became convinced that it was

*Love and a cottage! Eh, Fanny! Ah, give me
indifference and a coach and six!*

—George Colman

Miss Hannah Pym awoke, her heart beating hard. Her
dream had been so real, so vivid, that she lay very
still for a few moments, her eyes moving slowly
around the well-appointed bedchamber, already lit by the
pale light of dawn, reassuring herself that she was not in her
old room at Thornton Hall.

She climbed out of bed and began to dress hurriedly, but
all the time worrying about that dream. In it, she had never
been left a legacy by her late employer, had never had any
adventures on the stage-coaches or acquired a footman and
this elegant flat in the West End of London. In her dream, the
reality had been the dream, and she was once again Hannah
Pym, housekeeper, in black dress and cap, keys at her waist,
fretting about the amount of work she had to do. And there
in her dream had been her late employer's wife, Mrs. Clarence, pretty, laughing Mrs. Clarence, just as if she had never
run off with that footman; Mrs. Clarence who called, "Come,

Hannah, we have much to attend to. Just fancy Sir George marrying at last. We all thought him a confirmed old bachelor!"

The dream had been so vivid. Hannah felt she could still *smell* Thornton Hall, that mixture of beeswax and woodsmoke and dried rose petals.

Hannah shook herself like a dog as if to shake off the last horrible remnants of her nightmare. It was all in the past. Here she was in the present, about to embark on another journey, this time to York. For Sir George Clarence had reported that a friend of his had recently seen Mrs. Clarence in York, and that, combined with a desire to furnish Sir George with tales of more adventures, was taking her on her travels again. Hannah felt that Sir George could never love her: the difference in their social standing was too great. Although she was now a lady of independent means, Sir George knew her as his brother's ex-housekeeper. But he liked her tales of her journeys on the Flying Machines, as the stage-coaches were called, and Hannah had almost persuaded herself that his company on a few precious occasions was enough. Besides, there was Mrs. Clarence to think of, Mrs. Clarence who had been so kind to her. She might not yet know of the death of her husband, might not yet know that she was free to marry the handsome footman with whom she had run away.

"Benjamin!" called Hannah to her footman, asleep in the other room, and got a muffled reply, "Coming, modom."

Hannah Pym had no other servants. She had rescued Benjamin from the hangman on a previous adventure and he remained devoted to her. Many who saw Hannah, the thin spare spinster with the crooked nose, followed by her tall liveried footman, assumed she had a houseful of servants, for only the very rich could afford footmen.

"Come along, Benjamin," shouted Hannah, fearing he had gone back to sleep. "The coach leaves at six-thirty and we've got to get a hack to take us to Holborn."

"Ordered the bleedin' tumbril last night," roared Benjamin, whose accents swung wildly between common and refined, and the doctor who lived in the flat upstairs banged his chamber-pot on the floor in protest at the noise.

Hannah finished dressing and crammed her hat on her head and flew into the sitting-room where Benjamin, in shirt-sleeves, was laying out a dismal breakfast. Benjamin, thought Hannah, would never be a domesticated animal. His idea of breakfast was a loaf of bread and a pat of butter and a kettle that had only just been set on a spirit-stove.

"Leave it," snapped Hannah. "The hackney will be here any moment. We will get breakfast on the road."

Benjamin muttered something and went off to put on his new spun-glass wig and his livery which he had bought second-hand in Monmouth Street and which consisted of a red plush coat ridiculously embellished with gold epaulettes and embroidery, red plush breeches, and frilled shirt. He grabbed hold of his silver-topped walking stick and announced he was ready at the same time as the hackney driver could be heard howling from the street outside, prompting the doctor above-stairs to batter on the floor with the chamber-pot again.

When they got to the George and Blue Boar in Holborn, from where the coach was to depart, Benjamin paid the previously agreed hackney fare of two shillings. The driver promptly demanded five shillings and threw down his hat and said he would fight Benjamin for it. Hannah told him to be off or she would call the watch and pushed Benjamin towards the York stage-coach.

It was called the Stamford Regent and stood ready with four chestnuts harnessed up, shifting and restless, tossing their manes and sniffing the morning air. Ostlers, whistling through their teeth, were giving the last polish to the horses' flanks. In a doorway the coachman, Tom Tapton, who fancied himself a ladies' man, was talking to a pretty housemaid with her hair still in curl-papers. Ostlers began to shove luggage in the boot. The boot seemed to have an insatiable appetite and swallowed up everything thrown into it. Benjamin was being allowed to travel inside instead of with the outsiders on the roof. A thin, cadaverous man climbed aboard and took his seat. He had a colourless, epicene face and silver hair tied at his neck with a black ribbon. His eyes were pale blue and rested curiously on Hannah and then turned on Benjamin.

Then there came a rumpus from the inn yard. Hannah, ever inquisitive, let down the glass and looked out. A slim, female figure was standing waiting while her luggage was placed in the boot. Around her, insults rose in the air, cleverly not directed at her, merely polluting the air about her.

"Wonder if their women eats frogs," said one ostler.

"Can't tell wiff them Frenchies," jeered another. "Got dirty 'abits, they 'as. Should be killed like rats."

The girl's sensitive face was pale and drawn. Hannah assumed, rightly, that she was French and the butt of the French-hating inn servants.

She stepped down from the coach, holding her formidable umbrella like a club.

"Are you travelling alone?" she asked the girl.

The girl threw her a look, half-scared, half-pleading. "Yes, madame."

"To York?"

"Yes."

"Then you had better have a chaperone. You are French?"

A timid nod.

"Come with me. You need protection."

Hannah helped the young lady into the coach and into a seat beside her. "I am Miss Hannah Pym," said Hannah, holding out her hand, "and this is my footman, Benjamin."

The girl took Hannah's hand and shook it. "Merci," she said softly. "I am Mees Yvonne Grenier. I . . ." Her eyes fell on the cadaverous man and widened in alarm.

He smiled, baring yellow teeth like fangs. "I am Mr. Smith," he said.

Hannah felt Yvonne relax at the sound of Mr. Smith's English voice. What had she expected? Someone French? Hannah's curiosity made her odd eyes, like opals, change from blue to green.

And then something happened, something so wonderful that Hannah completely forgot about her fellow passengers. For there, outside the coach window, and smiling in, was Sir George Clarence.

Outside the coach went Hannah again, blushing like sweet sixteen, eyes like stars.

Inside the coach, Benjamin sat, rigid, biting his fingernails. He knew of his mistress's love for Sir George and had wanted to do something to prompt a romance. So when the maid to one of London's leading gossips had been sent to spy on Hannah, her mistress believing Hannah to be Sir George's mistress and wanting confirmation, Benjamin had gleefully supplied that confirmation, hoping that malicious gossip would force Sir George to propose to Miss Hannah Pym or, failing that, prompt his mind to more tender thoughts than mere friendship. Now the footman thought he must have been mad. Such gossip might drive Sir George away completely. Perhaps he had come because he had heard it.

But when Benjamin looked out of the window it was to see the couple chatting amiably.

"How very good of you to come at this unearthly hour of the morning to say goodbye," said Hannah shyly.

"I shall miss you," said Sir George gallantly, and Hannah felt quite weak with happiness. "I shall look forward to hearing your adventures on your return. I brought you some little things for the journey. He handed her a square box. Hannah babbled her thanks. "All on board the coach," roared the coachman.

"Goodbye," said Hannah, holding out her hand. Sir

George swept off his hat and bowed his head and kissed the back of her hand.

Hannah floated on board the coach and took her seat. Tears of happiness were standing out in her eyes. "Let 'em go," shouted the coachman, "and look to yourselves." The ostlers flew from the chestnuts' heads, the four horses sprang up to their collars, the guard performed, "Oh, Dear, What Can the Matter Be?" on his bugle, and the Stamford Regent surged out of the inn courtyard.

"What's that?" asked Benjamin, looking curiously at the box on Hannah's lap.

"A present from Sir George."

"Open it up," said Benjamin eagerly.

Hannah undid the silk ribbon which was tied around the box and carefully stowed it away in her reticule. Then she lifted the lid of the box. It contained a small bottle of attar of roses, a gauzy scarf in rainbow colours, a pretty little fan with ivory sticks, and a guidebook to York.

Hannah unstoppered the bottle of attar of roses and dabbed a little behind each ear. She wrapped the scarf around her neck and then handed the box with the guidebook and fan to Benjamin for safekeeping.

Benjamin was pleased. He had been worried that Sir George might have chosen indigestion powders or a woollen comforter or something dreary in the way of a present. The rainbow scarf, he thought, was like Hannah's odd eyes of many colours, and the coach was sweet with the fragrant smell of roses.

The coach rumbled up Cow Lane and through Smithfield and then slowed to a halt as it was suddenly surrounded by cows on their way to Smithfield market.

They sat listening to the lowing of the cattle and the cries of the guard urging the coachman to "fan 'em," and the coachman replying grandly that he had never whipped a beast yet.

Then they were on their way again and soon arrived at

the famous Peacock at Islington with its wood-and-plaster walls, its three storeys projecting over each other in front, its porch roof propped by caryatides. Outside the old inn stood an ostler with a horn lantern—although the early-morning sun was shining brightly—announcing the names of the coaches as they arrived at the door in a sort of bronchial wheeze. There were about twenty coaches outside the door, as all the northern coaches made a point of stopping at the Peacock. There was such an outcry, such a clattering of hooves, such a trumpeting of bugles, slamming of doors, and stamping of feet on splash boards, that Hannah was quite deafened, and through the hubbub rose the voice of the ostler, like a herald with a cold in the head, announcing the coaches: the York Highflyer, the Leeds Union, the York Express, the Rockingham, the Truth and Daylight, and, of course, the Stamford Regent.

Waiters ran out with trays of rum and milk. Benjamin and Hannah gratefully drank theirs, for it was still early and the coach was cold, but Yvonne and Mr. Smith both refused.

Off they then rolled out of Islington and soon began the ascent to Highgate archway. The sun shone down in all its glory from a clear blue sky, and down below, London still slept under a pall of smoke.

Hannah was beginning to feel very hungry indeed. She knew they were scheduled to change horses at the Green Man at Barnet and hoped they might breakfast there. But when they got to the Green Man, it was to learn that they were not due to breakfast until Enfield Chase. Brandy and hot water were served, and this time Yvonne and Mr. Smith took some refreshment. Hannah, stealing a sideways look at her French companion, noticed that the hot drink had at least brought some colour to Yvonne's face. They had quite a wait, for their coachman, Tom Tapton, that Lothario of the Great North Road, was dallying with a serving maid, his beaver adjusted at a rakish glance, his melting glances fastened occasionally on his next team, already fuming in the traces, but mostly on the Barnet Hebe, who was gazing up at him in adoration.

Finally, he called, "Take your seats, gentlemen, please," just as if the whole party had dismounted from the coach, and climbed in a leisurely way up onto the box, chewing a sprig of sweet lavender given him by the maid. Just as they were about to move off, the coach door opened and a large man climbed in and sat down between Benjamin and Mr. Smith.

Hannah glanced at the newcomer and then her eyes sharpened. He was a commanding figure. He was over six feet tall, amazing in an age when the average height was five feet. He had thick chestnut hair under a low-crowned wide-brimmed hat, silvery-grey eyes, a proud nose and a firm mouth and chin. His clothes were plain, but, Hannah noticed, had surely come from the hands of one of London's finest tailors.

"I hope I did not keep you waiting," he said in a light, pleasant voice.

"I think our Romeo of a coachman would have kept us waiting in any case," said Hannah tartly. "If he is set on dallying with every female on the Great North Road, we shall never reach our destination."

"Ah, who can resist a pretty maid," said the newcomer. He smiled at Yvonne, who shrank a little towards Hannah. "Allow me to introduce myself. My name is Giles."

The others introduced themselves in turn, "French," said Mr. Giles, looking at Yvonne. He broke into rapid French. Yvonne let out a little gasp and said, "Pray, I beg you, sir, address me in English. I must 'ave the practice."

"Of course. Are you travelling alone, Miss Grenier?"

"No," retorted Hannah quickly, "I am Miss Grenier's companion. We travel together."

Mr. Smith looked amazed. "I could have sworn you both met at the inn for the first time!"

Under the cover of her shawl, Yvonne's small gloved hand found Hannah's and pressed it hard. "I do not know what gave you that impression, sir," said Hannah. "We arranged to meet at the coaching inn at Holborn."

"But she introduced herself to you on the coach," protested Mr. Smith.

"I was looking out for her, not having met her before," said Hannah blandly. "I am taking care of her at the request of her family. She politely introduced herself."

"An unusually un-English trait, to be so interested in your fellow passengers, Mr. Smith," commented Mr. Giles.

The pale eyes turned on him. "I am as English as roast beef," said Mr. Smith.

"But as you are curious," pursued Mr. Giles, "I will indulge you. Now, I am travelling to York to see a relative. What is the nature of your business, Mr. Smith?"

"I also am travelling to York to meet someone," replied Mr. Smith huffily. He took a small book out of his pocket and began to read.

Mr. Giles gave a faint shrug. "And you, Miss Pym? It is not often one meets a lady complete with liveried footman on a stage-coach."

"I am travelling for the sake of travel," said Hannah.

"On a Flying Machine?"

"Why not, sir? An inexpensive and comfortable mode of travel."

"Hardly that. I myself, had I the money, would prefer a well-sprung travelling coach of my own, with six prime horses to pull it."

Benjamin's eyes gleamed. He was addicted to gambling and had not rattled the dice since a disastrous loss at Rochester the month before. But he had always been lucky before that dreadful game. If only he could have a great win, a magnificent win, then perhaps he could persuade Miss Pym to remain in London instead of retiring to a cottage in the country to eke out her legacy. Of course, if she married Sir George, that would solve all.

"And you, Miss Grenier," Mr. Giles was saying, "do you also travel for the love of it?"

"Yes," said Hannah quickly. "I told you, she is with me."

"Relative?"

"Friend of the family," said Hannah crossly. "I already told you so, or rather Mr. Smith. I am very tired, sir, and do not wish to answer any more questions."

Hannah opened the box Sir George had given her and took out the guidebook and began to read. But she hardly took in a word. What was Yvonne doing on the coach, and why was she so frightened? The Terror was still raging in France. The Revolution had been no great thing, but after it was over, the massacres had begun. Yvonne was in England and had nothing to fear, but perhaps she did not know that, thought Hannah. Had she come over from France recently? Her English, although accented, was very good.

And what of Mr. Giles? His very air and ease of manner showed him a man used to command.

The coach rolled towards Enfield Chase, where Queen Elizabeth, when still a princess, used to love to hunt. But she loved finery as much as she loved hunting, to the considerable disgust of her twelve ladies-in-waiting, who found themselves pursuing the flying hart arrayed in white satin and seated on ambling palfreys. Fifty archers, too, had to be gloriously dressed, with gilded bows in their hands, scarlet boots on their feet, and yellow caps on their heads. Hannah, who read history books as much as she read guidebooks, wondered if they had ever caught anything or if the stag had heard them all coming from miles away.

The coach lurched to a halt and the passengers climbed stiffly down. Hannah drew Yvonne's arm through her own as they walked to the inn and said in a companionable way, "You will feel better when you have eaten, Miss Grenier. There is nothing like a good English breakfast. I do not want to pry, but I would like to remind you that you are in the country of the free now. No danger can come to you."

Except, thought Hannah crossly when they were seated at the round breakfast table and she saw the admiring look Mr. Giles was giving Yvonne, from Lotharios.

Yvonne was very pretty, reflected Hannah—for a Frenchwoman. Hannah was very English, and like most English, terribly suspicious of foreigners in general and the French in particular. But there was something appealing about Yvonne. She had an oval face and very large hazel eyes fringed with heavy lashes. Her mouth was small and sweet and she had an air of grace and delicacy and vulnerability.

Benjamin appeared to have taken charge of Yvonne's welfare and was summoning waiters in a grand manner to attend to Hannah and Yvonne before the other passengers.

"I know you," said Mr. Giles suddenly, looking at Benjamin, who was standing behind Hannah's chair. "You're the fellow who downed Randall at Rochester. I did not see you there, but I saw you put up a splendid fight in the middle of Berkeley Square."

"Why was your footman fighting in Berkeley Square?" asked Yvonne.

"Because them poxy toads o' footmen put me up to it," said Benjamin.

"That's enough," retorted Hannah crisply. "You may go and find your own breakfast, Benjamin." Benjamin sauntered off to the room where the coachman and guard were dining.

"What did he say?" asked Yvonne.

"Oh, it is a long story." Hannah buttered toast. "He is prone to gambling, and in Rochester he lost a great deal of money and entered into a prize-fight where the purse enabled him to pay his debts. The fight in Berkeley Square I do not know about, or prefer not to know. Benjamin is rather . . . unusual."

"And, of course, you are *the* Miss Pym," said Mr. Giles.

"How did you hear of me?"

"The report of the Berkeley Square mill was in the social columns, Miss Pym. You were described as Benjamin's employer. I also believe you to be a friend of Sir George Clarence."

"You are remarkably well informed, Mr. Giles," snapped Hannah. "Now may I eat my breakfast in peace?"

He smiled and leaned back in his chair. What was it the gossips were saying only the other day? That Sir George Clarence had taken a mistress and that the mistress was Miss Pym, she the proud possessor of the battling footman. He looked at Hannah Pym, at her thin spare figure, her odd eyes, her sandy hair, and her good but sedate clothes, and decided the gossips must be wrong. He could not imagine Miss Pym being anyone's mistress.

Hannah finished her meal, wiped her mouth on the table-cloth, and went out to the necessary house at the back of the inn.

"There is a very pretty garden out there, just off the courtyard. I noticed it when we arrived," said Mr. Giles to Yvonne. "Would you care to take a stroll before the coach leaves?"

Yvonne hesitated. She looked about. She seemed to decide it was all so safe and normal—the low-beamed inn, the chat of the diners, the giggles of the serving maids from the side room where the coachman was having his breakfast, and the cries of the ostlers from the yard.

"Just for a little," she said.

He came round the table and helped her to her feet. Together they walked out into the sunlight and then through a little gate that led off the inn courtyard. Early roses were rioting in the garden and blackbirds were searching for worms in the daisy-starred grass. Yvonne gave a little sigh of pleasure and removed the shawl from her shoulders and put it over her arm.

"A little oasis of peace in a desert of despair," said Mr. Giles.

Her eyes flew to meet his. "Who said that?"

"I just did. You looked like a little hunted creature which has found cover."

"You are a poet, monsieur."

"Not I."

She looked up at him nervously. He was so very tall and powerful. His shoulders were broad although his waist was slim, and his chestnut hair, very thick and tied with a cherry-red ribbon, glinted in the sunlight.

He opened his mouth to ask her how recently she had come from France and then decided against it. "I am amazed at your friend, Miss Pym," he said instead. "To travel such a distance *for pleasure*."

"I can understand that, I think," said Yvonne, looking about her. "It is so far away from everything here. So peaceful."

"So far from the tumbrils and the stink and the guillotine," he said, suddenly, for some reason, angry. "Do the fools who cried for liberty and equality know what hell they were setting in motion? Do they sleep well o'nights, think you?"

She shrank back, one gloved hand to her mouth.

"I beg your pardon," he said quickly. But she ran away from him, half-stumbling, her shawl trailing through the daisies on the grass.

He cursed himself for his clumsiness and, taking out a penknife, he cut two red roses and walked slowly back to the inn, where he presented one to Hannah and one to Yvonne.

"Thank you, sir," said Hannah, her sharp eyes darting from his rueful face to Yvonne's white one. She had returned just as Yvonne had come rushing in.

"Gentlemen, take your places!" came the cry.

Hannah decided to pass the next stage by thinking of Sir

George and luxuriating over his presents, and leave worries about Yvonne until they stopped for the night.

Mr. Smith tipped his hat over his eyes and fell asleep. Subconsciously, Hannah relaxed. She did not yet realize that it was Mr. Smith rather than Mr. Giles with all his questions who had created an uneasy atmosphere in the carriage. She pictured Sir George as he had looked standing in the inn yard, the way he had swept off his hat and kissed her hand. Hannah raised the gloved hand he had kissed and held it briefly against her cheek.

As the miles rolled by, her thoughts turned again to Yvonne. There would be no matchmaking on this journey, as there had been on all the others. The idea of the shy and frightened Yvonne making a match with the tall, handsome and assured Mr. Giles made Hannah smile. It was sad, but it was obvious that Mr. Giles terrified Yvonne.

For some reason, known only to the coaching companies and not conveyed to passengers, the northern coaches often left the road to make inexplicable detours. So the Stamford Regent left the road at a place called Saint Neots in Cambridgeshire to go around some paper mills which were situated in the middle of the flat countryside. The coach stopped at a wayside inn and the passengers climbed down. It transpired that the river Ouse had, as usual, flooded, and that half a mile of road which lay ahead of them was under water. An extra pair of leaders, ridden by a horsekeeper, would need to be put on.

The company were invited into the inn and to their surprise were told that, as was the local custom, the refreshments had all been supplied by the local people and there would be no charge.

On a table covered with a damask cloth were spread plum cakes, tartlets, gingerbread, exquisite home-made bread, and biscuits. Ales and currant and gooseberry wines were presented in old-fashioned glass jugs embossed with jocund figures. "These have all been presented by the local cottagers and farmers," said the landlord proudly, "and they'd be mort insulted if any's left behind."

The home-made wine was powerful stuff, and despite the blotting paper supplied by all the cakes and bread and biscuits, the party began to become quite merry. "The reason for this fare," said Mr. Giles solemnly, "is that the road is often flooded and the idea is to fatten up the passengers so that they may be strung together and floated across, like so many balloons."

Yvonne giggled and said no doubt they would all sink like stones. She appeared to have forgotten Mr. Giles's hard remarks about the Revolution and suddenly seemed determined to enjoy herself. When they had finished and were waiting for the coach, she said gaily she was going out to see if she could see the flood. Mr. Smith promptly got to his feet and said he would accompany her and the pair walked off.

"Too slow," said Mr. Giles, shaking his head ruefully. "No doubt our Mr. Smith is murmuring sweet nothings in her ear."

"It must be much further on," Yvonne was saying. "I cannot see a thing."

"But you will soon see your father, mademoiselle," said Mr. Smith. He had spoken in French. Yvonne gave a little cry and looked up at him, her eyes dilated with fear.

He caught her arm as she would have run away and, still speaking in rapid French, he hissed. "You do not know me? I am Monsieur Petit."

Now Yvonne's face went a muddy colour. There was only one Monsieur Petit and that was Monsieur Jacques Petit, the most merciless of inquisitors and judges on the Paris Tribunal.

2

We shall see Buonaparte the bastard
Kick heels with his throat in a rope

—*Swinburne*

All the horrors of the Revolution crept about Yvonne like an evil mist. The calm English countryside, the winding road, the cheerful sounds from the inn behind her, the very contrast of her present surroundings to the hell that was Paris, all accentuated her fear.

"You cannot touch me," she whispered. "You have no power here."

"I do not want to harm you," he said. "On the contrary, I am delighted to make your acquaintance, for I am travelling to York to meet your father."

"To kill him!" cried Yvonne.

"At his request."

"Never."

"I assure you," he said smoothly, "I speak the truth."

"But he has been working against you, was working against you and all you stood for."

"True." He took a pinch of snuff. "But he has seen the

16

error of his ways, and as he was one of the heroes of our glorious Revolution, we naturally wish him to return to Paris."

"He thought he was helping to create a new world," said Yvonne bitterly. "A world of freedom. And when the Terror started, he did what he could to help people escape from France, and I . . . I am *proud* of him."

"He was misguided in that he helped aristocrats escape the guillotine." Mr. Petit looked calmly out over the landscape of the country which Napoleon wanted to conquer.

"Aristocrats!" Yvonne rounded on him. "Aristocrats! That is what you would like people to think. But few aristocrats have been guillotined compared to the vast number of ordinary decent people. Our neighbour could not pay his butcher's bill, so he reported the poor butcher to you at the Tribunal, saying he was plotting against the regime. So you murdered the butcher, and the neighbour laughed and said that was one bill less to worry about. The people my father helped were ordinary members of the bourgeoisie like himself."

"Nonetheless," said Monsieur Petit, unruffled, "he wishes to see me."

"I cannot believe you." Yvonne looked wildly around.

"But you *will* believe your father?"

"Of course."

"Then here is his letter."

Yvonne crackled open the parchment. In it, her father, Claude Grenier, stated that his only wish was to work for the Revolution and to help his good friend, Monsieur Petit. She stared at it in dismay. She wondered whether the terrible events of the Revolution had turned her father's brain at last.

She silently handed it back to him. "So you see, mademoiselle," he said, "you are in danger. If you betray me, I shall betray you. You are the daughter of Claude Grenier."

"But he is not a spy," said Yvonne. "Why should he be under any threat from the English?"

"Because, my innocent, there are many friends of the English king who have lost their lives. Believe me, you and your father would be taken to the nearest jail. And do not be seduced by the seeming friendliness of these English. Underneath, they are savage brutes. Go to any public hanging and see the oh-so-happy English crowds at play and ask yourself if there is any difference. And this Miss Pym, I know she is a stranger to you. Let her remain so or it will be the worse for you."

"Coach!" came a cry from the inn.

Yvonne wheeled about and ran back to the coach. She felt sick and bewildered and wondered what on earth to do. Yes, her father had worked for the Revolution, and with a single-minded passion, before all hell had been let loose. He had planned and organized escape routes from France in case he and his fellow conspirators might have to use them. But he had had to use them finally to help friends and relatives escape the guillotine. He said he was only glad that his wife, Yvonne's mother, had died of consumption before the horrors of the guillotine had begun and that she had not lived to see the death of all their hopes for a brave new France.

He had arranged Yvonne's escape two years ago and she had been living with a French emigré family in Cavendish Square ever since. Then he had written to say that he, too, was now in England and living in York and begged his daughter to travel north to join him.

Hannah looked sharply at Yvonne when she climbed into the coach. The girl looked terrified, thought Hannah in amazement, and shot a furious look at "Mr. Smith." She assumed Mr. Smith had been making advances to the girl, despite his age and the whiteness of his hair, and decided when they stopped for the night to give young Yvonne some warnings about strange men.

Mr. Giles looked at Yvonne calmly from under sleepy lids, but he said nothing and showed no more inclination to pay her any attention. The coach set off at a brisk pace.

Hannah decided she did not like the atmosphere pervading the coach. There was an air of menace. She darted suspicious glances at Mr. Smith, who smiled back blandly and took out his book.

And then the Stamford Regent entered the flood-waters. At first it was exciting to look out and see a flat plain of shining water stretching on either side. And then the water got deeper and flooded into the coach. Benjamin quickly drew his knees up to his chin as the straw on the floor of the coach began to float. Modesty forbade the ladies from drawing their legs up under them but Hannah, finding her feet getting very wet, put them up on the opposite seat on one side of Benjamin and begged Yvonne to follow her example and place her feet on the seat on the other side of the footman.

The coach lurched abominably as the waters rose higher. A small wave lapped against Monsieur Petit's knees. He jumped a little and dropped his book into the water and muttered a distinct, "Merde!"

"Ladies present," said Mr. Giles easily. "Oaths in French not permitted, mon vieux."

Monsieur Petit cursed himself for his slip. He prided himself on his excellent English and wished he had spoken in that language to Yvonne. For he was sure it was the fact that he had been recently speaking in his own tongue which had prompted him to swear in it.

Now the fear was that the coach wheels might hit some hidden obstacle beneath the surface of the waters. The inside of the coach was awash. Despite putting her feet up, Hannah's skirts were soaked. There was a mocking cry from the roof, "Land-Ho!," and sure enough, the six horses pulled up a small rise and the waters fell behind them.

"Thank goodness for that," said Mr. Giles. "I was eagerly awaiting the arrival of a dove with an olive branch."

Benjamin gave tongue. "What is that whoreson of a coachee abaht, I asks yer? My good livery. Ruined. Shite!"

"BENJAMIN!" screamed Hannah.

"It's too much," he mumbled. "I'll kill the dimmed arse-face, and be dimmed if I don't."

"I will have words with you when we stop," said Hannah awfully.

The wretched passengers climbed down from the coach at Buckden, demanding fires to heat them and rooms to change in. But the luggage, on being lifted out of the boot, proved to be soaked through as well. The coachman, Tom Tapton, was handing over the reins to another coachman at Stilton, where they were to stay the night. There were no pretty maids at the inn at Buckden either, and so the reluctant passengers were cajoled back onto the coach with promises that they would soon be at Stilton, where all their clothes would be dried and pressed for them.

Stilton, the home of the famous cheese, was soon reached. The cheese was actually made many miles away but had been christened by Miss Worthington, who owned the Angel Inn and sold the cheeses at her door.

The Angel was a huge inn where over three hundred horses were stabled for coaching and posting purposes, for Stilton was one of the greatest coaching centres. The ebb and flow of traffic never ceased. All day long, coaches and post-chaises poured in and out of it, and at night the mail coaches thundered in from the north. To add to the commotion and row, Stilton was where the great droves of oxen were shod so that they could make the journey to London with ease.

Facing the Angel across the Great North Road was the Bell, an equally large hostelry and the Angel's rival.

The Angel lived up to its reputation as a fine coaching-and posting-inn. The weary passengers were shown to bed-chambers where large fires blazed, and bustling, efficient servants bore off the clothes from their trunks to iron them dry in the kitchen while their owners shivered by their bedroom fires wrapped in fleecy blankets.

Hannah was sharing a room with Yvonne, Benjamin with "Mr. Smith," despite that gentleman's highly undemocratic protests about sharing a room with a servant, and Mr. Giles had mysteriously managed to gain the largest and best room for his own use.

Yvonne sat silently by the fire, answering Hannah in monosyllables, until Hannah decided to leave matters until the girl had dined and might be more relaxed.

Their dry clothes were delivered to them and each began to dress, Yvonne using the bed hangings on the four-poster as a screen. In an age when women rarely bathed naked even when alone, no female of any refinement would strip off before another member of her sex.

"Thank goodness our hair is not wet," called Hannah and received a muffled reply.

"May I come out?" asked Yvonne. "Are you dressed, Mees Pym?"

"Yes," replied Hannah, thinking that it was that "mees" which gave Yvonne away. She was surprised the inn servants at Holborn had known the girl was French, for Yvonne spoke English very well, but on reflection decided they had seen her name on the list in the booking-office.

"Where did you learn to speak English?" asked Hannah.

Yvonne approached the blazing fire. "I had an English governess when I was small," she said, "and during my two years in London, I earned a little money giving French lessons to English ladies. They learned French from me and I perfected my English by listening to them."

"Where did you get that gown?" asked Hannah, admiring Yvonne's dress of sprigged muslin. It was not the material but the cut and stitching that made it exceptional.

"I made it myself. It is one of my few accomplishments." Yvonne gave a rueful laugh. "You see, we were all so determined to be equal after the Revolution. No parasites, even among the ladies. And so I was apprenticed while still quite small to a dressmaker."

"So that was *before* the Revolution," said Hannah sharply, "or the Bourgeois Uprising, as we call it here. So

21

your family knew it was coming and were prepared. Never say your papa *worked* for the Revolution."

"How could we imagine what would happen?" cried Yvonne passionately. "We were going to make the new France, where all would eat and none would starve. How could we imagine the bloodshed, the tumbrils, the heads in baskets?"

She sat down suddenly and began to cry. Hannah put an arm around her shoulders. "Now, then," she said bracingly, "all that is behind you now. What have you to fear? This is England!"

Yvonne managed a watery smile. "And that answers all problems?"

"Of course. What did that Mr. Smith say to you to so upset you?"

"Nothing," said Yvonne quickly. "Nothing at all. Shall we go downstairs to the dining-room, Miss Pym?"

"A moment," said Hannah, looking at the girl's delicate face and at the blueish shadows under her eyes. "I thought at first that Mr. Smith, despite his age, might have been making advances to you. But there was an air of menace when we got back on the coach before we reached the flood. I do not like him. I do not like him *at all*. Was he baiting you because you are French?"

Yvonne remained silent, her face turned a little way away. Poor thing, thought Hannah. Poor frail creature. So delicate. Not at all like our sturdy English misses. I shall find out later what the trouble is.

Aloud, she said, "Do not allow yourself to be bullied, Miss Grenier. In my experience, bullies scent fear. I shall let you into a great secret, if you promise not to betray me."

Yvonne wiped her eyes and looked up at Hannah curiously.

Hannah took a deep breath. The Grenier family, after all, had supported the Revolution because they wished equality for all.

"I have only lately become a lady of private means," said Hannah. "All my life, I had been a servant. My late employer left me a legacy. But as a servant, one learns much of the ways of the world. Before I rose to become housekeeper to the Clarences of Thornton Hall in Kensington, I was an ordinary housemaid. The housekeeper then was a Mrs. Warby, a massive woman much addicted to spite and gin. She used to torment me, to find fault. One day, when she was tipsy, she knocked over a vase and broke it, went to Mrs. Clarence and said I had done it. Mrs. Clarence sent for me and I can still remember the gloating look on that Mrs. Warby's face. I was in floods of tears, standing before Mrs. Clarence with my head bowed. And then I felt her arm about my shoulders and her soft voice begging me not to cry, her voice telling me that Mrs. Warby, not I, had lost her employ. Then Mrs. Clarence made me sit down, and told me she had it in mind to elevate me to the rank of housekeeper. "But you must stiffen your spine, Hannah," she told me. "If you are always afraid of those above you, you will encourage bullying. Bullies *sense* fear. So smile, and throw your shoulders back and look them straight in the eye. Very simple advice, Miss Grenier, but very useful. Shall we go to dinner?""

Yvonne smiled suddenly, her large eyes sparkling. "Amazing Miss Hannah Pym," she said. "You give me courage. *En avant!*"

The gentlemen rose to meet them as they entered the dining-room. Monsieur Petit was wearing much the same style of clothes as he had worn on the coach, but Mr. Giles was magnificent in evening dress, black coat with silver buttons, black knee-breeches, gauze stockings, and ruffled shirt. As the ladies sat down, the maître d'hôtel bowed low before Mr. Giles and said, "Dinner will be served in a trice, my lord."

"My lord?" Hannah looked amused. "Your fine clothes have elevated you to the peerage, Mr. Giles."

"Not Mr. Giles," said Monsieur Petit crossly. "His secret is out. He is recognized here. He is the Marquis of Ware who, for some dark reason, needs to travel incognito."

"No other reason but debt," said the marquis languidly. "The duns were after me."

Monsieur Petit snickered. "That diamond pin you are wearing in your cravat, my lord, would fend them off for a time."

The marquis's face suddenly became hard and stern and his silver eyes bored into those of Monsieur Petit as he put both hands on the table and leaned forward. "Do not be impertinent, sir, or I will drive your teeth down your throat."

"An' I'll help you," commented Benjamin gleefully from behind Hannah's chair.

Monsieur Petit cast the marquis a venomous look and then turned to Yvonne. "You must find the manners of the English very boorish, Miss Grenier."

"On the contrary," said Yvonne, looking directly at him. "I find the gentlemen of England courteous and charming and *safe*."

She has thrown down the gauntlet, thought Hannah, amazed. He is startled and furious, but she is not afraid.

"What were your first impressions of London?" asked the marquis.

"I came up the Thames past Greenwich on a ship," said Yvonne, smiling at him. She was no longer afraid of him. He was nothing more than an aristocrat in debt. "So much shipping! It looked to me as if a forest of masts was growing out of the river. And the river itself! So brown and muddy, with mist drifting over the surface. There were jetties which thrust out fifty paces into the river on either side. There was gleaming mud left by the ebb-tide. Oh, a jumbled impression of warehouses and docks, ship-building and -repairing yards, mean dwelling-houses, the iron carcass of a church being made for assembly in India, or so someone told me, and all the many canals with their ships leading into the river, giving the impression of streets of ships. The mist changed into yellow acrid fog as we approached London. I thought myself in Homer's inferno, in the land of the Cimmerians.

"I arrived in London on Sunday."

"Ah," said the marquis. "Our famous English Sunday."

"It all had the aspect of a large, well-kept graveyard," said Yvonne with a shiver. "Tiens! How frightened and lost I felt. Shops closed, streets almost empty. It was raining—small, fine, close, pitiless rain. Everything was dirty and impregnated with soot. In the livid smoke, objects were no more than phantoms, and London looked like a bad drawing in charcoal over which someone had rubbed a sleeve."

"But the family with whom you are staying no doubt made up for the gloom outside with the warmth of their welcome," put in Monsieur Petit.

"Indeed they did."

"Their name being . . . ?"

"What is it you English say?" asked Yvonne with a sarcastic inflection on the *you*. "Mind your own business."

Hannah noticed that the marquis was toying with his food. He seemed fascinated by Miss Grenier. Hannah's matchmaking pulses quickened. "You must find, Miss Grenier," said Hannah, now anxious to keep Yvonne talking, "that there are great differences between the English misses and the French."

"A very great deal, yes."

"Tell us," urged the marquis.

"The English misses are healthier, being addicted to riding and to walking. I teach some ladies French, and so have had the chance to observe their ways closely. I was surprised to find, for example, that it is rare to come across a fashion journal in any of the great houses. And the magazines they do read! No fiction, no chatty column of theatrical gossip, no fashion notes, none of the things you would find in a French journal. Instead, in one magazine for ladies, there was an article on education in the workhouses, one on slavery in America and its influence on Great Britain, and one on the improvement of nurses in agricultural districts. So the English misses are more intelligent. But they do not know how to use this intelligence. No one teaches them the art of conversation. Nor do they know how to coquette." Yvonne raised her fan and flicked it to and fro and then flirted over it with her eyes at Monsieur Petit, who stared at her angrily.

"Go on," said the marquis. "So young and so wise. You intrigue me."

"Everyone pays lip-service to love in this country," went on Yvonne, "and so husband-hunting is very vulgar. A rich and noble man is much run after. Too effusively welcomed, flattered, and provoked, he becomes cautious and is constantly on his guard. It is not so in France. Girls are kept under too much restraint to take the initiative; in my country, the game never turns hunter."

"But English women are faithful," said Hannah. "Marriage is a respected and noble institution. Someone once told me he had heard one Frenchman say casually to another, 'I hear your wife has taken a lover.' Things are managed better here."

"I do not think so," said Yvonne with a quaint old-fashioned air. "Your English mees has much more freedom before marriage than her French equivalent. But *after* marriage—and here I speak of the bourgeoisie, not of the lords and ladies—the husband is the head of the household and his wife must be quiet and submissive. They have families of eighteen children." She raised her hands. "And without shame!"

"Miss Grenier!" Hannah looked shocked.

"You frown then on legalized lust," teased the marquis. "Eighteen times is hardly an orgy."

Yvonne blushed. "Forgive me. I am too outspoken and it is not fair of you, milord, to underline that fact with coarse remarks."

"I humbly beg your pardon," said the marquis, his eyes

26

dancing. "You are about to tell us they organize things better in France."

"Yes," said Yvonne seriously. "For there the husband will discuss his business at all times with his wife. Here, she is kept in such ignorance so that, should he die, she has no means of taking up the reins of business herself."

"Perhaps Englishwomen should marry French husbands," jeered Monsieur Petit.

She gave him a cool look. "It does not always answer, for Englishwomen in business do not know how to charm. There is a French innkeeper at Calais with an English wife. He is all charm and has great interest in his customers, going from table to table to see they have everything they need. But the English wife! Ma foi! As the guests get up to leave, she calls out in execrable French, 'Havez vo' payez?' No ease of manner. No elegance."

"We are nonetheless," said Hannah stiffly, "a very moral people."

"On the surface," sighed Yvonne. "Very moral. Your very novels read like religious tracts. The fallen woman is always ugly and comes to a bad end, which is not always the case. All is clean and decent on the surface, but the Englishman in his cups can turn beast. Look only at the thousands of prostitutes who throng the streets of London, the houses in the Strand, the young girls of fourteen with babies at the breast. Pah!"

"My dear Miss Grenier," drawled the marquis, leaning back in his chair, "we do not drag hundreds of our countrymen to the guillotine to have their heads chopped off."

"No, my lord, you just hang them seven a side on the gallows-tree outside Newgate."

"After a fair trial, Miss Grenier."

"Yes." Her face grew sad. "Yes, I forget the horrors at home. I have drunk too much wine and that has led me into the rudeness and folly of criticizing my hosts."

"We English are so arrogant," said Monsieur Petit, "that no criticism can dent our smug armour."

"Spoken like a true Frenchman," said the marquis softly, and Monsieur Petit shot him a startled look.

A newcomer strode into the dining-room and looked around the assembled company through his quizzing-glass. His face brightened as he obviously recognized Monsieur Petit. "Well, Jimmy," demanded the newcomer, "how goes the world?"

Hannah was startled. Whoever would think that the cadaverous and sinister Mr. Smith would answer to the homely name of Jimmy? The newcomer was a young man, foppishly dressed, rouged and painted and padded, with a large black patch in the shape of a coach and horses on one cheek-bone. He had small, watery brown eyes and thin brown hair, backcombed and teased until it stood up on his head, giving him an air of perpetual surprise.

"My friend Mr. Ashton," said Monsieur Petit. "He will be travelling north with us. Mr. Ashton, allow me to introduce our little company. Miss Pym, Miss Grenier, and the most noble Marquis of Ware."

"Servant," said Mr. Ashton laconically. "Word with you in private, Jimmy."

Monsieur Petit rose and the pair went out together.

"Into the yard," urged Monsieur Petit. "We will not be overheard in all the bustle. How did you arrive?"

"Mail-coach. Just got in."

They strolled into the yard of the Angel.

"So, monsoor," said Mr. Ashton, "how goes the game? I see the Grenier female is travelling under her own name. What's a marquis doing on the stage?"

"He says he is running from the duns."

"A marquis? Never. Lords can live on tick until the day they die. But he can't be after you. Not anything to do with the War Office or anything like that. In fact, he's the kind who would look better with his head in a basket, eh?"

"Keep your voice down," snapped Monsieur Petit. "What possessed you to call me Jimmy? Do I look like a Jimmy?"

Mr. Ashton shrugged. "Seemed a good English name to me. What d'ye want me to call you? Pierre? Where you learn the lingo anyway?"

"My mother was English."

"Was? Chop her head off, hey?"

"Listen, you cur," said Monsieur Petit savagely, "you are being paid well for your help. One more word of insolence from you and I will abandon the project, and before I leave this perfidious country I will shop you to the authorities."

"Two can play at that game," said Mr. Ashton, quite unruffled.

"Where did our embassy find such as you?" demanded Monsieur Petit angrily.

"I do anything for money," said Mr. Ashton, stifling a yawn. "Not murder, but anything else. Do not exercise yourself, Monsoor Frog. You are on the right coach. Have a word with the girl?"

"Yes, I showed her a letter from her father to me which he wrote before the Revolution. She does not know that and is convinced her father now wishes to help us."

"And when she finds we mean to follow her to him and take him back to France at gunpoint?"

Monsieur Petit smiled slowly. "She will do nothing. She goes with him as well."

"Such a pretty neck, too," said Mr. Ashton. "Ah, well, I've been paid the first half and very generous your people were, too. What's the drill?"

"Just make sure she does not give us the slip and leave the stage-coach at any point before we get to York," said Monsieur Petit.

"Right," Mr. Ashton nodded. "And what about Lord Thingummy?"

"A lazy penurious aristocrat? I would we could take him as well. How many of his tenants, think you, had he beggared before he ran into debt?"

"As long as he's no threat, then he can beggar the lot, for all I care," replied Mr. Ashton. "That's the trouble with your lot. Always hot and bothered about something."

3

It is not easy to persuade an Englishman to talk about his illicit amours; for many of them this is a closed book the mere mention of which is shocking.

—Hippolyte Taine

Mr. Ashton was to travel with them, much to Hannah's dismay, for she had taken the young fop in dislike. He began by letting the other passengers know that he thought he was a cut above stage-coach travel. There was enough straw on the floor, he said acidly, to hide a whole covey of partridges, and he kept picking bits of straw fastidiously from his clothes.

Monsieur Petit added his complaints. He could not understand why inns did not offer napkins to the guests, so that they had to wipe their fingers and mouths on the table-cloths, and he considered the custom of offering slippers to new arrivals a filthy one. He had refused to wear them. You never knew who had worn them last.

Yvonne looked out at the passing scene and tried to forget the presence of Monsieur Petit and his friend. A good night's sleep, not to mention the bracing company of Hannah Pym, had done wonders for her spirits. The more she thought about that letter, the more she became convinced that it was a fake, or rather a fake in that Monsieur Petit had pretended to have recently received it. Perhaps it was one her father had written to him *before* the Revolution, for her father had been friendly with him then, that she knew. Monsieur Petit wanted her to keep her distance from Miss Pym. Well, she would not. There was something comforting about Hannah's strength and the amusing devil-may-care cockiness of her servant, Benjamin. Yvonne wondered whether to confide in Hannah. For when she got to York, she had no intention of leading Monsieur Petit to her father, not until she had seen her father first, and she felt that Hannah might offer help in enabling her to slip away.

She turned her eyes from the landscape outside and met the silvery-grey eyes of the Marquis of Ware. There was an oddly speculative look in his eyes. Her senses sharpened by danger, Yvonne began to worry about him for the first time. He did not look down at heel. He had given up the pretence of being Mr. Giles and was now dressed like a marquis. She saw enemies everywhere and prayed for the day when they would arrive in York. Her father was brave and resourceful. He would know what to do. But Mr. Petit *did* frighten her. She shivered and Hannah pressed her hand. Yvonne gave her a shy smile.

Mr. Petit caught that smile and had noticed that press of the hand. Something would have to be done about Yvonne Grenier before they reached York. Then there was the upsetting presence of the Marquis of Ware. His clothes had undergone a change. He seemed to be making no effort to appear impoverished. He would discuss the situation with Mr. Ashton when they stopped for the night.

Hannah Pym looked out at the passing scene but with diminished enthusiasm. As they rumbled their way through towns and villages, heads popped out of casement windows to survey the one excitement of the day—the sight of the Flying Machine.

York suddenly seemed a long way away, much longer than its one hundred and ninety-nine miles from London, almost at the edge of the world. The monotonous creak, creak, creak of the coach was beginning to get on Hannah's nerves. She began to feel like a jaded traveller whom nothing can surprise. A tinge of homesickness crept in on her. What on earth was she doing in this still-damp coach travelling to the ends of the earth when she might be in her little flat in London, awaiting the arrival of Sir George?

But perhaps she might come across Mrs. Clarence in York and that would be worth any discomfort, any long and tedious journey. Just thinking about someone other than herself always cheered Hannah, and so her thoughts turned easily from Mrs. Clarence to Yvonne Grenier. There was something badly wrong with this coachload, rumbling its way northwards in the failing light; a marquis who had claimed to be ordinary Mr. Giles; and a Mr. Smith who frightened Yvonne and who had been joined by his foppish friend, Mr. Ashton.

By the time the coach jolted its way into Grantham, where they were to spend the night, Hannah had decided to question Yvonne further.

Here was an attractive French girl and here was an aristocrat, and a very handsome one, too. Of course he might be as impoverished as he claimed to be, although Hannah, wise in the ways of the world, knew an aristocrat's idea of poverty was a far cry from that of the wretches of the rookeries in London. If there was something about Mr. Smith to fear, then perhaps that might rouse the knight-errantry in the marquis. Feeling quite warm from all these interesting speculations, Hannah alighted with the others at the Bull and Mouth in Grantham.

The Bull and Mouth was not only a coaching-house but a posting-house as well, which meant it catered for a grander type of customer, and coach passengers were usually relegated to a small dark pit of a dining-room at the back of the inn. Thanks to the magnificence of the Marquis of Ware, they were ushered into the main dining-room and a good bill of fare was set before them instead of the usual repast of pork in various shapes and sizes.

Monsieur Petit decided to use the supper-time to find out what he could about Miss Pym. If that spinster lady were to get too close to Miss Grenier, then he wanted to know whether she was a creature of consequence who would make a difficult adversary or a pretentious woman who was aping her betters by having some relative dress up as a footman.

Over the soup, he fixed her with his pale eyes and asked, "You are from London, Miss Pym?"

He got a brief nod in reply.

"Which part of London?"

"The West End," replied Hannah with a faint lift of her eyebrows, as if to imply that such as she could hardly be expected to live anywhere else.

"It is odd to see a lady accompanied by a footman on the stage-coach," pursued Monsieur Petit. "Particularly a footman who is allowed to travel inside."

Hannah smiled but did not offer any explanation.

"I have never travelled on the stage before," said Mr. Ashton pompously. "Usually take m'own carriage."

"And what brought you on the stage this time?" asked the marquis.

"Heard my friend Mr. Smith was bound north, so decided to join him."

A large roast fowl was placed before the marquis. He carved off the wings first and offered them to Yvonne. The wings were the favourite part, something that was to drive Lord Byron into sulks, for he could never understand why such delicacies should be given to the ladies. Yvonne indicated Hannah, but Hannah refused, saying she preferred a slice of the breast instead.

Monsieur Petit had been racking his brains as to how to

find out more about Hannah. "The Season will soon be over," he volunteered.

"Do you not regret missing it?" asked the marquis with a cynical gleam in his eye. "Are not the ladies pining at ball and saloon, asking where, oh where, is our Mr. . . . er . . . Smith?"

"You jest, my lord. I do not frequent the Season. But Miss Pym, surely . . . ?"

He allowed his voice to trail off and looked at Hannah encouragingly.

Hannah smiled at him again and again did not reply.

To Mr. Petit's annoyance, there was an interruption. A fashionable party entered the room, an elegant man with a finely dressed lady and two young girls. The lady saw the marquis and sailed forward, hand outstretched. "My dear Ware," she carolled. "What are you doing in this common inn?"

"Like yourself, I am travelling, Lady Abbott. Allow me to make you known to the company."

Lady Abbott held up one gloved hand. Her large eyes surveyed the group. "That will not be necessary," she said, her tone, slightly amused, implying that the marquis's company was beneath her notice. "Do come and meet my daughters," she said.

The marquis gave a sweet smile and raised the carving knife. "My apologies, Lady Abbott. As you can see, I am too busy engaged in carving this fowl. Do you dine?"

"We have a private dining-room."

"So what brings you to the common dining-room?"

"My maid told me some fantastical story that you had arrived on the common stage. I found it scarcely credible, but now . . ." Her eyes raked over the company. "Oh, here is my husband. You know Abbott, of course. My daughters, Indiana and Philadelphia." Both girls curtsied.

Hannah found herself becoming very angry indeed. Hannah Pym, friend that she was of Sir George Clarence, should be accorded proper respect, not snubbed by this Abbott female. What made it even worse was that Lady Abbott was not going out of her way to be nasty. She obviously believed the company to be beneath her notice. Hannah nervously fingered the corded silk of her own gown.

Yvonne looked wide-eyed at Lady Abbott. She was a handsome woman in a tamboured gown, her oiled head ornamented with feathers. Her daughters, both in their late teens, were gazing up at the marquis with well-trained adoration. In looks, they were neither of them out of the common way, but they had been schooled to please and find husbands. Hard work removes pretty innocence, thought Yvonne. I could never gaze at any man with that cowlike look of worship.

"Pray join us," said Lord Abbott.

"How can I join you," said the marquis mildly, "when I am obviously otherwise engaged?"

Lord Abbott half-turned his face away, but his words were perfectly audible. "But such company! I assume you are travelling on the stage for some lark."

Benjamin had heard enough. He considered Hannah had been slighted. "My mistress's food is getting cold, so why don't you all go away," he said loudly.

"Are you addressing me?" Lady Abbott raised her quizzing-glass.

"Yes, I am," said Benjamin, unrepentant. "Move along, do, my lady." He raised his voice to a mincing falsetto. "I'Faith, I was never so bored in all my life."

"You outrageous whipper-snapper," raged Lord Abbott. "I'll have you horsewhipped. You . . . madam"—to Hannah—"kindly curb your servant."

"Indeed I would, my lord," said Hannah coldly, "were it not that I agree with every word my Benjamin says."

Indiana promptly swooned. It was gracefully done, for she had spent hours in front of her glass perfecting the art, but the Marquis of Ware did not catch her. That task was left to Benjamin. Indiana opened her eyes and said weakly, "Oh, my heart," found Benjamin grinning down at her and struggled free with a squawk.

"I see now," said Lady Abbott, struggling for calm, "why it is, Ware, that you have elected to go on the common stage." She made it sound like acting in the theatre. "Obviously your travelling companions suit your low taste."

Pushing her twittering daughters before her, she flounced off, followed by her husband, leaving the marquis and the rest.

The Marquis continued to carve. The others sat silent, all engrossed in their unhappy thoughts. Monsieur Petit was grinding his teeth and thinking that Lady Abbott would be considerably improved in appearance were her head in a basket in front of the guillotine. Mr. Ashton was ruffled. He considered himself no end of a dandy, but Lady Abbott's insults had brought back to him unwelcome memories of many such slights. Hannah was depressed. She had so lately been a servant that she felt sure the stamp of the servant class was marked on her face for all to see. Yvonne had met many such ladies as Lady Abbott when she visited the houses of the rich in London to teach French. Somehow, she had not particularly minded before. She had been too grateful for the work. But the horrible Lady Abbott had made her feel small and shabby and undistinguished.

"Such a pushing, vulgar creature, that Abbott female," said the marquis meditatively, looking around the gloomy faces. " 'Tis said her father was in trade."

All the bruised egos turned to him like flowers to the sun. Hannah began to laugh. "Did you but mark her daughter's outrage after she had manufactured that swoon only to recover in the arms of Benjamin?"

The others laughed as well and, in one brief fleeting moment, the odd assortment were united by a communal dislike of the high-handed Lady Abbott.

But then Monsieur Petit remembered his mission and reflected that the presence of this marquis was becoming increasingly irritating. He was obviously well known, and no innkeeper on the road would forget their visit. Mr. Ashton covertly studied Yvonne. She was a neat piece of work, he thought, fiddling with a goose quill to prize a recalcitrant piece of chicken from between his teeth. He rather fancied himself as a ladies' man. Perhaps he could flirt with her, dazzle her, and so make her blind to any danger. So ran his conceited thoughts while the object of them looked around the stable security of the dining-room of this English inn and became more determined than ever to ask help of Miss Hannah Pym. This was not Paris, where one learned quickly not to trust anyone but a few close friends, and menace lurked around every street corner. She felt a pang of envy for the marquis. He was eating neatly and deftly, looking relaxed and amused. He was handsome and burnished and tailored to perfection. She did not believe his tale of poverty. He was armoured by birth and fortune and looks against a world of poverty and danger, snubs and deception. He had only to raise his head and look about him for the waiters to come running, not in the hope of a good tip, but because he was "my lord." The landlord hovered near the table as well, eyes sharp for any sign of slackness on the part of his staff.

A large log fire crackled on the hearth and the branches of candles on the tables burnt clear and bright. Yvonne felt a lump rising in her throat caused by a craving to be part of this secure world.

Conversation became desultory, and as soon as the meal was over, they all decided to retire to their rooms. Yvonne was to share a bedchamber with Hannah. Both ladies walked up the shallow polished wooden treads of the inn staircase, a waiter walking before them with a candle to light their way.

"What it is to be in the company of a marquis!" exclaimed Hannah as they entered what was obviously one of the best bedchambers in the inn. A coal fire was burning brightly, and beeswax candles burnt on the mantelpiece instead if the usual tallow ones.

Both ladies worked busily, opening their trunks and looking out their night-rail and clean clothes for the morning.

"And now," said Hannah in the same matter-of-fact voice she had just been using to praise the comforts of the bedchamber a moment before, "perhaps you might enlighten me, Miss Grenier, as to what is going on? I have never found myself among a stranger group of passengers, and there is an air of secrecy, furtiveness and, yes, menace emanating from our Mr. Smith and his foppish friend, and I think you know why."

Yvonne gave a little sigh and sat down suddenly in a small armchair by the fire and looked at her hands. Hannah waited patiently.

"I was going to tell you," said Yvonne at last. "I had made up my mind to ask for your help. Mr. Smith is in fact Monsieur Petit of the Paris Tribunal. He told me that my father had written to him saying that he, my father, who had turned against the Revolution, was now in favour of it, and wished to return to Paris and help the new regime. He showed me a letter. It is in my father's handwriting, but I am convinced now that it is an old letter, one sent before the Terror began. He wishes to either kill my father or to take him back to Paris by force to stand what passes for a trial in that unhappy city."

Hannah sat down in a chair facing Yvonne and said seriously, "We must have a council of war."

Yvonne moved her shoulders in a Gallic shrug and her pretty mouth drooped with disappointment. The seemingly capable Miss Pym was merely an over-romantic spinster.

She gave a brittle laugh. "Really, Mees . . . Miss Pym, would you call the British generals to our aid?"

"No, no, but we shall have my Benjamin in to hear your story, and the Marquis of Ware."

"Milord? But why? He, I am persuaded, would find the whole thing most distasteful, and in his roast-beef English way he would turn the whole lot of us over to the nearest magistrate."

"And what would be so wrong with that idea?" Hannah's eyes flashed green.

"My father is living, perhaps incognito, in York. But if the English knew he was Monsieur Claude Grenier, he who helped so much in the cause of the Revolution, they might take him as a spy." She shivered. "I see enemies everywhere."

Despite her concern for the Frenchwoman's plight, Hannah's busy matchmaking mind was working furiously. Yvonne was of the French bourgeoisie, which put her well below the level of an English marquis, not to mention a French one, if, thought Hannah bleakly, there were any of that breed with their heads still attached to their bodies. But a maiden in distress worked wonders with even the most hardened cynic.

"A marquis has great standing," said Hannah aloud. "Let us have him in, and if he shows the slightest sign of calling the authorities, I, Hannah Pym, will order a postchaise and take you off to York myself this night and they will never catch us. Trust me, Miss Grenier."

Yvonne looked this way and that as if seeking escape. She wished now she had kept her troubles to herself. She thought of the very small amount of money she carried with her. There was no way she could hire a conveyance for herself and escape. Better to go along with Miss Pym's plan.

She finally nodded reluctantly. Hannah went in search of Benjamin and asked her footman to find Lord Ware and to bring him to their bedchamber.

Yvonne waited nervously by the fire. The sound of carriages arriving and departing came up from the courtyard below. She looked up as the door opened. The flames of the candles streamed out in the draught as the marquis and Benjamin walked into the room.

The marquis executed an elegant bow. "It is not often,"

he said airily, "that I have the honour of being invited by *two* ladies to their bedchamber."

Yvonne's heart sank. Here was a man who knew nothing of violence or danger or treachery. Women to him were pretty playthings, or some sort of boring lesser race, but nothing else.

But it was too late to draw back. Hannah gravely outlined Yvonne's problem.

The marquis listened with every appearance of calm interest, while behind his handsome face his mind worked furiously. He had been sent by the War Office to find out what this Monsieur Petit was doing in England. Instead of picking him up, they had decided to have him watched. The fact that they had found out that he had booked a seat on the York stage under the name of Mr. Smith had really sparked their interest. The marquis had done valuable work before. He had protested against using an alias, saying that one fake on a stage-coach was surely enough, but the authorities had pointed out that a marquis travelling on the stage might in itself be enough to frighten off Monsieur Petit, and then they would never learn what he was up to or what he was about to get up to. But he had no intention of telling anything of this to the assembled company. Yvonne naturally thought only the best of her father. But if Monsieur Grenier showed any sign of returning to France to assist that murderous regime, then he must be stopped. The French were devious. Had not this upstart Napoleon tricked everyone, including his own people, by claiming that all he wanted was peace for France? Had he not just led his vast armies into the plains of Lombardy and taken over northern Italy? Certainly it seemed odd, with all Napoleon's greater plans, that the French should wish to go to great lengths to drag back from England one bourgeois gentleman to stand trial, and yet that was how terror kept its grip on a people. Always punish the "traitors" and in as public a manner as possible to keep everyone else in line.

He smiled and said lazily, "It's as good as a play. But if you want to get rid of this Monsieur Petit and his unsavoury friend, why, it is simple."

"How?" demanded Benjamin from the shadows.

"I will tell the coachman that our friends do not wish to continue their journey and tell the innkeeper that they are not to be roused. I will buy their seats and persuade the coachman to leave an hour earlier."

Hannah looked at him, disappointed. "By, my lord, all they will have to do is hire a post-chaise and catch us up on the road."

"My little mind did think of that." The marquis stifled a yawn. "At the next stop, it is we who will hire a fast carriage and so proceed to York."

"For an impoverished aristocrat, you still seem to have a great deal of money," commented Hannah wryly.

He smiled. "Nothing is too much to please a lady. Now, Miss Pym, if you and your footman would like to retire for a short time, I wish to have a word in private with Miss Grenier."

"But, why?" Hannah stood protectively next to Yvonne. "We are all in this. It is not the thing to be alone in an inn bedchamber with a young lady, or had you forgot?"

"I am well aware of it, ma'am, but no one need know except yourself and Benjamin. Pray indulge me."

"I am used to taking care of myself," said Yvonne quietly.

Hannah left reluctantly, followed by Benjamin. "Ten minutes," she called over her shoulder, and then closed the door behind her.

The marquis took a seat opposite Yvonne. The candlelight gleamed in his thick chestnut hair and his silvery eyes scrutinized her. "Tell me, Miss Grenier, why you trust your father?"

"He is a good man. He risked his life saving many from

42

the guillotine. He never thought the Revolution would turn into such a cauchemar."

"When did you last see him?"

"Over two years ago. He smuggled me out of France and gave me letters to friends in London. I quickly found work." She smiled bitterly. "England may be at war with France, but all the English ladies want is to learn French."

He studied her for a few moments, noticing the haunted expression in her large hazel eyes. "But surely the parade to the guillotine has ceased."

"They are no longer dragged there daily in their hundreds," commented Yvonne dryly, "but Madame La Guillotine is still kept tolerably busy."

There was a long silence. Yvonne wondered what this marquis was thinking. His next question startled her. "Do you have a beau in London?"

"Moi? Tiens! I teach French and mend the gowns of the ladies I teach for a little extra money. Who would court such as I?"

"Strange. I would have thought you would have many admirers."

"Ah, that is different. There are young men in some of the households I visit and they can become a trifle tiresome. But what of you, milord? You ask so many questions and give nothing in return." Her large eyes sparkled. "What of your amours?"

"Englishmen never talk of such, Miss Grenier."

"Oh no? Unless they are in their cups and with other gentlemen and then they talk and talk and talk. Par example, I was in the house of Lady Jedder, non? She has some sewing for me, what she calls 'a little present,' which means she is paying me over and above the price of the French lessons but less than she would give a seamstress. Lord Jedder is talking to his friends and they walk into the library. They see me, or don't see me, for I am of the rank of servant and such do not exist, non? So they talk freely, Lord Jedder has had his way the night before with a certain lady, a widow, but of good *ton*. He not only tells his friends this but describes the how, the why, and the wherefore in great detail. So after that, there was a certain milord in another house who wished to steal a kiss from me. He was very attractive and I had never been kissed, *vous voyez*. But I immediately thought how he would gossip and so I ran away."

"And so are you still kissless?" asked the marquis, like any true aristocrat dismissing the rest of her discourse and retaining the one bit that interested him.

"Yes."

"And when and how do you plan to lose your . . . er . . . lips?"

"When I marry—*if* I marry."

"Oh, I am sure you will."

Yvonne wrinkled her brow. "It is not so easy. I will, if I marry, choose one of my own countrymen. But I have only saved such a little bit of money, and without a dot—a dowry—such things are difficult."

"Had you known Miss Pym before?"

"No. I met her for the first time on the stage-coach. I decided to confide in her because she appears so courageous. Now I feel I might have made a mistake."

"How so?"

"Eh bien, I was dismayed when she insisted on enlisting your help, milord."

"A very sensible thing to do. Have I not said I will arrange your flight?"

"Y-yes," she said doubtfully. "But it all seems to you like a game, and to me it is a matter of life or death."

"Here comes our Miss Pym. Do not trouble, Miss Grenier. We shall soon leave your villains far behind. I will tell the waiter to call you at four-thirty. We leave at five."

Hannah entered with Benjamin at her heels and he repeated the arrangements before bowing himself out.

"I am worried," said Yvonne as soon as the door had

closed behind the marquis. "What if this marquis is working for the French? He says he is short of money."

"I think that was a hum," said Hannah.

"But this Mr. Ashton, he is with Monsieur Petit and *he* is English."

"But Ashton's a loose fish," commented Benjamin.

"He means that Mr. Ashton is the type to gravitate to any sort of unsavoury company for money," explained Hannah. "You will find that Lord Ware is highly respectable."

Yvonne sighed. "But so frivolous. Here I am in fear of my life and my father's life and all he can do is ask me if I have any beaux."

"How interesting," said Miss Hannah Pym. "How very interesting."

When they all assembled at the coach at five in the morning, having had a mere half hour to wash and scramble into their clothes, Hannah expected some sort of protest from the coachman, but he and his guard were all smiles and bows. The marquis must have paid them heavily, thought Hannah.

They had gone a little way up the Great North Road when they came to a steep hill and, as was customary, the marquis and Benjamin got out to walk to lighten the load. Benjamin kept looking anxiously over his shoulder. Their pace was so slow, he feared that the Frenchman and his friend would soon catch up with them. At this pace and having only gone this short distance from the inn, Monsieur Petit had only to run to catch them up.

The marquis, wrapped in a greatcoat with many capes and with a wide brimmed hat pulled down over his eyes, appeared lost in thought.

He suddenly called up to the coachman. "Is Hadley Hall not near here?"

"Lord Trant's place?" called down the coachman. "'Bout a mile up the road."

"I have changed my mind," said the marquis. "Take us there and then you will still be in time to return to the inn for that couple we left behind and any other passengers."

"But that's not what you paid me for," cried the coachman, fearful that the marquis would ask for his money back.

"You may keep what I paid you," said the marquis, "only do not breathe a word to anyone of where we have gone."

The coachman gave him a broad wink, and as the coach had reached the top of the hill, he told the marquis and Benjamin to 'op inside.' The coachman was sure the marquis and Yvonne were eloping.

"Now," said the marquis, once he was seated inside the coach, "there is a change of plan. Lord Trant, who is an acquaintance of mine, has a seat near here. I suggest we go there and stay today and tonight and set out for York in the morning. By that time, our pursuers will not know where to look. There is one problem. Did your father mean to meet the coach, Miss Grenier?"

Yvonne shook her head. "He sent me directions to his home. It is within walking distance of the Bell, where the York coach was to set us down."

"Nonetheless," said the marquis, "I feel you should write him a letter and give it to me. I will send one of Trant's servants to Grantham with it to catch the mail."

Yvonne looked doubtful.

"Come, you are wondering whether to trust me with your father's address. Give the letter to the servant yourself."

"But are you sure Lord Trant is in residence and will welcome us?"

The marquis smiled. "He has two marriageable daughters. I shall be very welcome."

"Then how are you going to explain *our* presence?"

"I have French relatives. Miss Grenier is my cousin and you, Miss Pym, are an English friend of the family."

Hannah was too gratified to protest. "Friend of the family" pleased her immensely. She would have been cast down if he had planned to describe her as a family servant or even chaperone.

Yvonne's face was white. She was tired and longed to see her father. She dreaded having to stay for even a short time in a household of strangers.

"You can sleep all day," said the marquis, as if reading her thoughts. "You do not even have to leave your room if you do not wish to do so."

The coach lurched to a stop. Hannah could hear the coachman calling out to a lodge-keeper and the lodge-keeper replying in a sleepy voice. Then there came the grating sound of iron gates being opened and the coach moved forward.

The estates appeared to be large because it was some time later before the coach stopped again, this time in front of a huge sprawling mansion.

The passengers climbed stiffly down, Yvonne and Hannah feeling as if they had been miles on the road instead of travelling only a short distance.

An efficient butler answered the door, as majestic in his night-gown as he probably looked in his livery. Not by one flicker did he betray that he thought it extremely odd of the Marquis of Ware to arrive in a stage-coach at dawn, saying he had come on a short visit.

The butler led them through a large square hall and into a saloon on the ground floor where they drank coffee and admired the peacocks strutting on the terrace outside in the dawn light while the butler went to rouse the housekeeper and get their rooms prepared.

"Is he not going to tell Lord Trant we are here?" asked Yvonne nervously.

"No need," said the marquis laconically. "I am always

welcome. One of the benefits of being a bachelor with a title."

So much for my matchmaking dreams, thought Hannah. This handsome lord is too far above Yvonne—and too much in demand!

Once a woman has given you her heart you can never get rid of the rest of her.

—Sir John Vanbrugh

Hannah lay in bed awake and listened to the early-morning silence of Hadley Hall. She had been so sure that sleep would come immediately that she had eagerly fallen in with the marquis's suggestion that she and Yvonne should retire to bed, after Yvonne had written that letter to her father.

Yvonne herself had handed it to a servant, concealing the address from the marquis as she did so, which Hannah now restlessly thought was rather silly, considering that the marquis had only to ask the servant when he returned what it was.

During her years as a servant Hannah had been used to rising very early in the morning and it was a habit she could not break. She secretly felt her inability to sleep late was a common trait and had been sure that her new status of gentlewoman would soon permeate her whole body. But she was wide awake with her thoughts. Yvonne had said she would probably keep to her room all day, but Hannah had no intention of letting her do so. That young lady should spend as much time in the company of the Marquis of Ware as possible. Hannah herself had every intention of presenting herself to their hosts.

And then she was in the drawing-room and Sir George Clarence was there. Hannah gave a glad cry and moved to join him, but he raised his quizzing-glass and stared at her appalled. "Who is this creature?" he cried. And from behind Hannah came Yvonne's anguished voice, "Miss Pym! You have forgot to put on your gown." Hannah looked down, and sure enough, she was clad only in her petticoat. She let out a cry of dismay and sat up in bed, unable for the first few horrified moments to believe it a dream. Although her dream or nightmare appeared to her to have been of short and horrifying duration, the sun was now high in the sky. Hannah climbed down from the high bed, feeling superstitiously that God had sent that dream to warn one ex-housekeeper who was getting socially above herself.

She pulled the curtains, which had been open only a little, fully back, opened the casement window and leaned out. The air was warm and sweet and fresh. Down below was a terrace with scarlet and white roses tumbling down from ornamental stone urns. A table with a white cloth had been set on the stone flags of the terrace, and at the table were seated a group of people: a silly-looking lady with a vapid face, two younger ladies—her daughters?—and a plump red-faced man.

The door opened behind Hannah and Yvonne walked in. She joined Hannah at the window.

The older lady's voice carried up to them. "Well, Trant, I roused our gels as soon as I heard he was here."

The group then was obviously comprised of Lord and Lady Trant and their two daughters.

"After all," went on Lady Trant, "there is no denying

Ware is a splendid catch. Why has he not married? He must be in his thirties."

"Amuses himself too much," wheezed Lord Trant. "Opera dancers and the like."

"Remember the delicate ears of our daughters, Trant!"

"Sorry. But Ware is as rich as Croesus, so it stands to reason he don't need to marry until he feels like it."

Yvonne put a hand on Hannah's arm. "He said he was poor," she hissed.

"I never really believed that, you know," replied Hannah, "and I'm sure you didn't either."

"Then why was he really travelling on the stage?"

Hannah was sure now that the marquis had been doing it merely for a wager or for some other equally frivolous reason. She was wondering how to reply to Yvonne without lowering the marquis in that young lady's esteem when, down below, Lady Trant spoke again.

"He is not alone, I gather. He has people with him, and both female. What are they like? Chubb is not good at descriptions."

"How can I tell?" demanded his lordship testily. "I ain't seen 'em yet."

"What are their names?"

"Ware gave his card and a servant could hardly demand to know the names, lineage, and background of the women. Ware merely said something about the young one being a cousin and t'other a friend of the family, that's all. Chubb says they all arrived on a stage-coach, but that butler of ours gets older and deafer and dafter by the day."

One of the daughters gave voice for the first time. Hannah could see little of her, for she was wearing a wide-brimmed straw hat. "He didn't even look at Clarrie and me in London." The voice was high and petulant. "If you ask me, he's merely using our home as a hotel."

"Well, I ain't so high and mighty as you, Letty," said the

one called Clarrie in a surprisingly deep voice. "I say, let's have a go at him now we've got him under our roof."

"And how can you 'have a go at him,' as you so vulgarly phrase it, sister dear?" demanded Letty sweetly. "*I* have a folio of water-colours to show him, not to mention entertaining him by playing the harp. What have *you* to offer?"

"Show him the gardens," said Clarrie. "All gentlemen like gardens."

Hannah drew back from the window. "I confess to finding myself a trifle hungry, Miss Grenier," she said. "Perhaps we should descend."

"I will have something sent up on a tray to my room," said Yvonne.

Hannah thought quickly. "That will not do, you know. Your hosts would find it most odd if you did not put in an appearance."

"I will say I have the headache." Yvonne looked stubborn.

"And what a waste of time that will be on this fine day," said Hannah bracingly. "And you in that old carriage gown. Do you not have a pretty muslin? The day is warm."

"I have a sprig."

"Then put it on! I can lend you a fine shawl. Come, Miss Grenier. It is necessary for both of us to talk to the marquis further and find out what plans he has made for conveying us to York."

At last Yvonne reluctantly agreed and soon she and Hannah were descending the main staircase. A footman met them in the hall and led them through a saloon and out onto the terrace where the Trant family, now joined by the marquis, were seated at table.

The marquis rose and made the introductions. At first Lady Trant and her daughters only had eyes for Yvonne. Hannah thought Yvonne was looking very pretty and appealing and hoped the marquis thought so too. Yvonne was wearing a white muslin gown embroidered with little pink sprigs. It had a low neckline and puffed sleeves. Over it, she wore the brightly coloured shawl Hannah had lent her. Around her white neck was a simple necklace of seed pearls. Her hair was dark brown with little gold lights shining in it and dressed in a clever style; a knot of curls on top of her small head. Hannah noticed that Yvonne's hair, although it was free of pomatum, shone with a silky light, and made a mental note to ask her what she put on it.

"We are but recently come from London," Lady Trant was saying. She began to talk of various notables while Hannah accepted tea and a plate of ham and kidneys. Yvonne listened dreamily to the rise and fall of voices while she gazed out over the sweep of the lawn. The soft air smelt of roses, newly cut grass, tea, and ham. She was unaware of the curious looks being cast on her face and gown by Clarrie and Letty. Both Clarrie and Letty were wondering whether to further their suit with the marquis by being pleasant to her, or whether to regard her as a rival. What sort of cousin? A first one, which put marriage out of the question, or a distant one, which made her dangerous?

Lady Trant had been discoursing on the merits of the latest play she had seen when she suddenly stopped and stared full at Hannah. Her rather vacant face appeared to harden and grow lines under the shadow of the enormous cap she wore on her head. "Miss Pym," she said slowly. "Miss *Hannah* Pym. Of South Audley Street?"

Hannah inclined her head in assent.

"Are you acquainted with Sir George Clarence?"

Benjamin had just appeared and taken up his position behind Hannah's chair. He gripped the back of the chair hard.

"Why, yes," said Hannah with a pleased smile.

Lady Trant cast a look of horror at the marquis. "Lord Ware," she said stiffly, "much as we are pleased to entertain *you* in our home, we have our daughters to protect, and causing themselves to be brought into contact with a member of the demi-monde is beyond the pale!"

"What's this?" goggled Lord Trant.

"I fear your wife has been listening to malicious and unfounded gossip," said the marquis coldly.

Hannah found her hands were trembling and clasped them firmly on her lap. She fixed Lady Trant with a baleful look and said in a level voice, "Explain yourself, my lady."

"*You* ask *me* to explain *myself!*"

"This could go on forever," said the marquis with a sigh. "Miss Pym, I heard the rumour and did not believe a word of it. The gossips are saying that you are the mistress of Sir George."

Hannah's sallow skin turned a muddy colour. "But there is no foundation for such a rumour. None! It is spite and envy. Sir George is a courteous and . . . and . . . kind gentleman. I am outraged."

"If it is such a lie," said Lady Trant in a thin voice, "then why did the gossip start with your own footman, Miss Pym?"

"That's a bleedin' lie," screamed Benjamin suddenly. "I never did!"

"Silence!" ordered the marquis. "Lady Trant, Miss Pym is a close friend of mine. I also know Sir George Clarence. I can assure you that there is no truth in the rumour. Nothing but scurrilous lies. Of course, if you prefer to believe the scandalmongers, then I fear I must remove my cousin and my friend from Hadley Hall so that neither may be subject to further insult."

Yvonne, who had been looking in a dazed way from one to the other, nonetheless marked that the usually easy-going and laconic marquis looked formidable.

"Well, *I* don't believe a word of it," said Letty quickly. "I mean, just *look* at Miss Pym!"

All looked at spinster Hannah, at her good and fashionable clothes, at her outraged eyes, at the prim spinsterish set of her figure. Lady Trant flushed slightly. "Well, dear me, Miss

Pym, now I come to think of it, and considering what one knows of Sir George and having met you, of course the whole thing is ridiculous. Pray accept my sincere apologies."

Hannah gave a stiff little bow from the waist by way of acknowledgement. Clarrie got to her feet. "Pray allow me to show you the gardens, Lord Ware," she said. "It is such a fine day."

He smiled and rose as well and soon could be seen walking slowly away across the lawns beside the dumpy and energetic figure of Clarrie. "I shall go too," said Letty quickly and ran after the pair.

In a rather stifled voice, Hannah said she wished to retire for a little. Lady Trant was all solicitude, promising to send her own lady's-maid up to attend on Miss Pym, apologizing over and over again at having bruised "so distinguished" a guest's feelings.

"Come, Benjamin," ordered Hannah.

Lord and Lady Trant followed them out. Yvonne, still eating breakfast, stayed where she was. The sun was warm and pleasant. She felt she should go after Hannah and see if that lady needed any soothing down after the insult that had been given her, but then decided against it. The formidable Miss Pym was made of iron and Lady Trant had certainly apologized.

Her thoughts turned to the marquis. He had reached the edge of the lawn. Clarrie appeared to be trying to pull him one way and Letty the other. Clarrie was squat and ill-favoured with a masculine voice, Letty was tall and thin and flat-chested, but both were the daughters of a lord, with all the background of wealth and privilege. Yvonne began to feel very low. A man such as the marquis would never look in her own direction. Not that she wanted him to, she reminded herself quickly. She did think that he was probably wealthy and had lied about his poverty. No poor man could have bribed a stage-coach driver or offered to pay for a post-chaise to York. He was not escaping his debtors by getting on the coach under an assumed name. Therefore, it followed, he was probably escaping from some amour. A large cloud floated high above and cast a shadow on the grass and some of that shadow seemed to enter Yvonne's soul. She finished her breakfast and went in search of Hannah.

In Hannah's room, the angry spinster was facing her footman. "You *what?*"

"It seemed like a good idea at the time," mumbled Benjamin. "I mean, I thought, like, Sir George needed a bit of a nudge in the direction of marriage. I thought he would feel obliged to make an honest woman of you, so ter speak."

Hannah clutched her head in despair.

"You meddling fool! Now I can never see him again. What have you done to me, you jackanapes?" A wave of grief and loss for her ruined dream swept over her and she sank down into a chair and dabbed at her now streaming tears with a handkerchief.

"I meant it only for the best," said Benjamin in anguish. "You won't want me now. I'll take meself off."

Hannah scrubbed at her eyes and then shook her head. Benjamin was like a member of her family, almost like a son. She could not tell him to go.

"I feel it is a judgement on me, Benjamin," said Hannah wearily. "I have been getting above myself. All these adventures with lords and ladies and getting on familiar terms have quite gone to my silly head. Sir George would never marry me or even think of me in any terms warmer than friendship. It is probably as well this has happened. Give me some time alone to recover. But do not ever try to meddle in my affairs again. Do I make myself clear?"

"Yes, mum," said Benjamin, anxious to get away from her before he too broke down and cried.

When he had gone, Hannah opened her trunk and took

out a flat box. In it lay the spoon she had taken from Gunter's, the famous confectioners, to commemorate the times they had taken tea there. Beside it lay the glove he had kissed.

They would need to be thrown away. Her heart would mend the quicker if she kept nothing to remind her of Sir George. Into the box she placed—as if placing a small corpse in a coffin—the bottle of scent he had given her. This was followed by the scarf, the delicate little fan, and the guide-book.

She swallowed convulsively and then rang the bell. A trim housemaid answered it and Hannah handed her the box, "In here," she said in a choked voice, "are some items I no longer need. You are welcome to them."

The housemaid bobbed a curtsy and took the box. Out in the passage she met Benjamin, who was hovering about. "What's that?" asked Benjamin sharply. He bit his tongue hard to repel another bout of sobbing and repeated, "What's that?"

The housemaid hugged the box to her bosom. "Your mistress done give it me."

"Let me see."

Reluctantly she opened the box. Benjamin looked sadly down at the contents. "Buy it from you."

"Them's mine!" The maid tossed her head and set the streamers on her cap bobbing.

Benjamin fished in his pocket and extracted two sovereigns and tossed them up and down. "Gold," he said.

Sunlight shining through a long window in the passage glittered on the coins.

Her eyes gleamed. "Very well," she said breathlessly. Benjamin handed over the coins and seized the box and ran off with it to stow it in his luggage. Somehow, he must think of a plan to repair the damage he had done.

That afternoon, the marquis sat at a desk in his room. He had given the excuse that he had letters to write, in order to escape from Letty and Clarrie. He knew they were waiting below for him in the drawing-room. Letty had promised to play the harp.

And then, looking down from the window, he saw Yvonne crossing the grass, a light breeze fluttering the thin skirts of her gown. She had heard the angry voices from Hannah's room and had decided to go for a walk.

He left his room and darted quietly down the stairs and looked for a moment out across the empty lawn in front of him before he remembered that the window of his room overlooked the lawn at the back of the house. He quickly made his way there, fearing every moment to hear the patter of feet as Letty and Clarrie ran after him. As he reached the back of the great mansion it was to see Yvonne opening a tall ornamental iron gate which led to a walled garden.

When he entered the garden himself, he saw her standing by a sundial in the centre and went to join her. The garden was a mixture of flowers and herbs. The air was warm and heavily scented. Trim box-hedges separated the beds in an Elizabethan pattern of shapes: clubs, hearts, and diamonds.

Yvonne turned and saw him and smiled and he caught his breath. "It is very safe here," she said simply. "My grand-mother has a house in Brittany, near the coast, with a walled garden. This reminds me of childhood and security."

Something stirred in him. She looked so delicate and fragile and yet so gallant that he wanted to present her with the security she craved. She moved on down one of the paths and he fell into step beside her. "Tell me," said Yvonne, "of this scandal about our Mees . . . Miss Pym. You appeared to know all about it."

"Miss Pym is evidently the friend of a dry-as-dust retired diplomat." Oh, how Hannah's heart would have ached could she have heard him describe the love of her life in such terms. "Some jealous cat put it about that Miss Pym was this Sir George Clarence's mistress. I knew of the tale when I first met Miss Pym on the stage-coach, but one has only to look at her to know, to realize what rubbish the story is. But Lady Trant had the right of it in that it is believed the story originated with her own footman. Her Benjamin looked stricken enough at the breakfast table."

"So what will happen now? What will this Sir George do?"

"If he has tender feelings for Miss Pym—which I doubt—he may propose marriage. If not, then, old diplomat that he is, he will no doubt find some excellent way to scotch the rumour. But what of your troubles, Miss Grenier? What happens after I have conveyed you safely to York?"

Yvonne smiled slightly. "You may say goodbye to me and my troubles. My father will arrange all."

His glance glinted at her. Was she being devious and very, very clever? There was always a power struggle in any political scene. If her father was still regarded as one of the original heroes of the Revolution, Petit might have been telling the truth in that Monsieur Grenier meant to return to France. In that case, he might prove a formidable rival and Petit's plan could indeed be to get rid of him. His clever daughter could be using himself and Miss Pym as cover until she got to York so that she and her father could escape to France unscathed and there help to perpetuate that monstrous regime of terror. She was not like any female he had ever known. He knew where he was with English misses, who barely used any finesse in their pursuit of him. There was something mysterious about Yvonne and yet he dearly wanted to believe her innocent. A peacock cried harshly from outside the garden like a warning from a harsher, more brutal world.

"I should return and see how Miss Pym fares," said Yvonne. "Can it be that she loves this Sir George?"

"Hardly." The marquis laughed, as if the very idea of such as Miss Pym in love were totally ridiculous.

"Age is no barrier against love," said Yvonne quietly.

"That you should understand, milord, being perhaps nearer to Miss Pym's age than my own."

"You are right." He was suddenly annoyed. "I am beyond the age of puppy love."

"Then that you should convey to the two young ladies of this house," said Yvonne tartly. "It would save them wasting their time."

"I did not mean I would not marry," he said.

"So you would marry without love?"

"I think mutual rank, fortune, and a certain amiability are better foundations for marriage than love."

"It is possible, I think, to have all those things and love as well."

"You being an expert on the subject."

"Me being an expert on the subject," she agreed.

"How so?"

"I was affianced at the age of sixteen to a Monsieur Paul Charlot. We were very much in love." Yvonne sighed and the marquis found himself becoming furious. "What happened?" he asked in a carefully neutral voice.

"Eh bien, with Papa turning against the Revolution and using most of our fortune to help people escape, marriage was no longer possible."

"Why? Did this Paul support the Revolution?"

"He was neither for it nor against it, being of a gentle, retiring disposition. But I no longer had any dowry, you see, so naturally he had to find someone else."

"Jackanapes. Mercenary puppy," snapped the marquis.

"But affairs are organized here in the same manner," said Yvonne. "Hardly ever does a man of any substance marry a penniless girl."

"And you accepted the situation just like that! Without complaint?"

"Oh, I am of a practical turn of mind. I cried a great deal, of course, but," went on Yvonne with a certain amount of pride, "only when I was alone. I kept my dignity."

"But you said you had never been kissed! Such a sweet and tender love and no kisses."

"It is not the same in France," said Yvonne primly. "French girls are not so forward as English ones."

She stopped to sniff a rose and he looked down at her, half exasperated, half amused. "Would you like me to kiss you?" he asked abruptly.

Her eyes flew to meet his and she coloured faintly and then automatically veiled them with her long eyelashes, a coquettish gesture. "But why?"

The answer was, thought the marquis suddenly, "Because I think I might be a little in love with you," but he said aloud, "For amusement. Would you not like to have the experience?"

Those eyelashes raised. "Perhaps," she said slowly. "For it would not matter. After York I will not see you again. Yes, perhaps I will try." She turned her face up to his.

He cradled her face in his hands and gently kissed her on the mouth. Someone in the house had started to play the harp—Letty—and he felt suddenly as if the very angels were serenading them. Such innocence, he thought in a dazed way, such piercing sweetness near to pain. The sun was warm on his head and the scents of herbs and roses mingled with the scent from her hair. And then a black wave of passion seemed to crash across his brain and the next thing he knew, she was struggling free of his lips, looking up at him, wild-eyed and frightened.

"I am so sorry," he said huskily. "I did not mean to frighten you." But she turned and ran away from him, through the flower-beds, and out of the gate.

Benjamin was riding to Grantham on a horse he had borrowed from the stables. In his pocket was a letter to Sir George Clarence. Feeling that the damage had been well and truly done, Benjamin thought that he may as well explain his folly to Sir George.

> *Dear Sir George [he had written], By the time you Receive this Letter, a scurrilous Rumour concerning you and my Mistress, Miss Pym, may have reached your ears. I was the Instigator of that Rumour. It was my belief you had a tendre for my Mistress and I was aiming to help the Course of True Love.*
>
> *Alas! My Mistress found out what I had done and is in Tears and says she can Never see you again. What am I to do?*
>
> *Pray accept the Apologies of one Grief-Stricken footman who remains Yr. Humble Servant, Benjamin Chubb.*
>
> *Ps. One my return to London, you may Horsewhip me, an it please you,*

Benjamin had laboured over a dictionary in the library to make sure his spelling was correct. At Grantham, he left the letter to be collected by the next-up mail coach and went into the tap of the Bull and Mouth to refresh himself with a pint of dog's nose before returning to Hadley Hall.

The innkeeper recognized him and hailed him with surprise saying there had been no end of a to-do when those two gentlemen, Mr. Smith and Mr. Ashton, had found the party had gone.

"So what did they do?" asked Benjamin.

"Hired a post-chaise and set off hell for leather," said the innkeeper.

Benjamin smiled. At least that would be some good news to take to Miss Pym. But then Miss Pym would ask him what he had been doing in Grantham and he could not possibly tell her he had written to Sir George.

He sighed, feeling all the weight of a guilty conscience bearing down on him again. His drink—a mixture of beer and gin—began to make him feel slowly better. The taproom was dark compared to the blazing sunshine outside. Smells of cooking were drifting through from the kitchen to mingle with the smell of sweating horses from outside, as carriages came and went. He called for a newspaper and retired with his tankard to a table near the door where an oblong of sunlight shone on the flags. Benjamin sipped his drink and read slowly. He was reluctant to return, to see Hannah's sad face. He promised himself that he would go as soon as he had finished the paper, which was a London one, only a day old. And having made that promise, he settled down to read every line, ending up with the obituaries. With amazement and relief, he read that Lady Carsey, his old enemy and tormentor, she who had threatened to get revenge on Miss Hannah Pym as well as himself, had died. With more amazement did he note that she had died of a heart attack. He would have expected such a cruel and violent lady to have died a more fitting death. He folded up the newspaper and tucked it into his pocket. He would show it to Miss Pym but would not tell her where he had come by it.

Yvonne found Hannah in her room. The spinster was sitting in a chair by the window, very still, her hands folded on her lap.

"You were very distressed about the gossip," said Yvonne. "But what is gossip?"

"A dreadful weapon," replied Hannah quietly. "I had no hope, you see, not at any time, for how could such as Sir George look on me in that light. But while we were friends, I could dream. Now my dreams are gone."

"Sir George," said Yvonne tentatively. "Was he not the handsome gentleman with the white hair who gave you the presents before we left London?"

"The same."

"Miss Pym, he looked at you with such affection. If any gossip maligned a friend of mine, I would not believe a word of it, and it would not alter that friendship."

"I am an ex-servant." Hannah looked weary. "And it is a scandal in itself for Sir George to entertain me."

"But that did not prevent him from doing so, non? How did he entertain you?"

Hannah's odd eyes grew misty as she remembered each precious moment. "He took me to Gunter's, twice, to the opera, and showed me the improvements to the gardens at Thornton Hall."

Yvonne's quick and pragmatic Gallic mind fastened immediately on the most important point. "He took you to the *opera*?"

Hannah nodded.

"Then, believe me, madame, he doesn't give a fig for public opinion. His . . . er . . . feelings of friendship must be very strong indeed."

"Well, I am sore embarrassed." Hannah's square shoulders rose and fell in a gesture of resignation. "Best to forget him. I gave all mementoes of him to a housemaid."

Yvonne fell silent, but her mind was working busily. She thought of the marquis and a little colour rose to her cheeks as she remembered that kiss. How violent her own emotion had been! And was she not in the same position as Miss Pym? Such a man as the marquis had been merely dallying with her. But Miss Pym must be helped. She, Yvonne, must fight down her embarrassment, go on as if that kiss had never happened, and ask the marquis to talk to Sir George on his return to London.

"Are you going to stay in your room?" she asked.

Hannah shook herself and her eyes flashed green. "No, I am not. I have decided that this journey is to be my last adventure. I shall retire to somewhere quiet in the country and no more will I have the opportunity of being entertained by lords and ladies, so I plan to make the most of this. There is the dressing-bell. They keep country hours. Let us put on our finest, Miss Grenier, and amuse ourselves by watching the young ladies in hot pursuit of our marquis!"

They assembled in the drawing-room before dinner, which was to be served at four in the afternoon. There was no sign of Benjamin, and Hannah hoped her mortified footman had not run off and left her. Letty and Clarrie were seated on a sofa on either side of the marquis, curls bobbing, faces animated as they vied for his attention. The marquis raised his eyes and looked at Yvonne, a long, enigmatic look, and she quickly veiled her own eyes, feeling her heart beginning to thud.

The marquis led Letty into dinner, Letty being the elder daughter. Conversation at the table was mostly led by Lord Trant, who talked endlessly about crops and fertilizers. Yvonne felt her head beginning to ache. All at once, she longed to be with her father and away from this disturbing aristocrat with the silvery eyes who made her heart beat so hard, and made her lips ache with the memory of that kiss.

But after dinner, there was a long time ahead, during which Letty played the harp and displayed her portfolio of water-colours and Clarrie looked at her with raging jealousy.

Benjamin had returned, but after one sharp look at him, Hannah had ordered him to bed. She was sure her footman was thoroughly drunk, although he was trying gamely to conceal it.

After a game of Pope Joan, supper was served, and after it, Yvonne, with relief, saw Hannah rising to retire for the night and prettily thanked Lord and Lady Trant for their hospitality. The marquis said he had ordered a carriage from Grantham to collect them at six in the morning. He kissed Hannah's hand but only gave Yvonne the briefest of bows.

A little of Hannah's misery was beginning to ease as she

thought about the journey to come. York lay ahead and perhaps somewhere in York was Mrs. Clarence, and if only she could find Mrs. Clarence, Hannah felt that would go a long way towards easing the grief she felt over the loss of her dreams about Sir George.

Quit, quit, for shame, this will not move,
This cannot take her.
If of herself she will not love,
Nothing can make her.
The devil take her!

—Sir John Suckling

Long shafts of dawn sunlight streamed through the park of Hadley Hall as the marquis, Yvonne, Hannah, and Benjamin left for York. Mist was coiling around the boles of the trees, birds were carolling, the well-sprung coach swayed gently, and each one of the travellers began to feel that life might hold promise after all. It was a rare English summer morning, fresh and perfect, heavy with the scent of flowers and grass. Out on the road, bowling past fields of corn, through the golden veils of rising mist, it was hard for Yvonne to think of darkness and danger. Villainy, like all bad things, belonged to the night.

She voiced this thought aloud and the marquis's eyes glinted with amusement as he murmured, "Not *all* bad things." Yvonne flushed and looked down. Hannah glanced quickly from one to the other, her matchmaker's senses quickening.

"I meant to ask you, Miss Grenier," said Hannah,

"what pomatum you use on your hair. It is so soft and shiny."

"Nothing but soap and water," replied Yvonne.

"You *wash* your whole head?"

"Certainly."

"But have you not considered the dangers? Dampness permeating to the brain? Neuralgia? Toothache?"

"There is no danger unless you sit around with wet hair in a draught," said Yvonne.

Hannah poked at her sandy hair under her bonnet. She had given up washing her hair, considering it to be a rather common thing to do. Besides, refined ladies were delicate and subject to ills which servants, being of a coarser fibre, escaped. Refined ladies *never* washed their hair, thought Hannah, forgetting in her anxiety to be a real lady that a great part of the British population neither cleaned nor washed their hair at all.

She usually cleaned her hair by brushing fuller's earth through it and sponging it with cologne. Perhaps when they stopped next she would wash it and it might have some of the lustre of Yvonne's. And Sir George might perhaps admire . . . But Sir George would no longer be part of her life. The sun continued to shine outside. Smoke rose in thin columns from cottage chimneys. But inside Hannah's soul, a darkness settled down again. To console herself, she thought of Mrs. Clarence. Once Yvonne's problems were solved, she would stay a few days in York and see if she could find that lady.

But as the miles flew past, her spirits began to rise again and her natural optimism to take over. Benjamin gave an exclamation and pulled that newspaper from his pocket and handed it to her, pointing to the obituary. He had hitherto been very quiet, knowing that his correct place was on the backstrap outside but feeling that if he did not remind the marquis of his presence, then he could stay inside in comfort.

Hannah read the obituary notice and sighed with relief.

"Well, Benjamin, there's an end to her and I can only wonder that she died in her bed."

Intrigued, Yvonne pressed her for an explanation and so Hannah settled back and told Yvonne and the marquis about the wicked Lady Carsey, she who had tried to have Benjamin hanged for a crime he had not committed and who had pursued them to Portsmouth and had tried to drown them. How the terrible twins, Lord William and Lady Deborah, had pretended to be Hannah and Benjamin, risen from the dead, and had frightened Lady Carsey out of her wits.

And for the rest of that day, until they arrived at their last overnight stage on the road, Yvonne pressed Hannah for more tales of her adventures while Benjamin beamed with pride on his mistress and silently prayed that Sir George would find some way to make things all right.

Courtesy of the marquis, they all put up for the night at a posting-house which was too grand to accommodate mere stage-coach passengers.

They took their supper in a private parlour. The marquis said they should start early and they would be in York in the morning. "And then what?" he asked, his eyes resting on Yvonne. "Do we take you to your father?"

Yvonne shook her head. "I am most grateful to you, my lord, for all your help, but I will go to my father alone."

"Is that wise? Petit and Ashton will be scouring York for you."

"I can take care of myself," said Yvonne with a little sigh, and he wanted to say that *he* would take care of her, but felt he could not. He was not ready to commit himself to anything on the strength of that one kiss.

Hannah visited Yvonne in her bedchamber before they retired for the night. The marquis's generosity had meant separate bedchambers. Yvonne was sitting in front of the toilet-table, unpinning a fichu from her dress, "I came to bid you good night," said Hannah, "and to beg you to reconsider your decision to go to your father alone. Would you not be better with the protection of Benjamin or Lord Ware?"

Yvonne shook her head. "It is better I go on with my own life and not see my lord again. But if you will give me your direction in London, I shall write to you and let you know what happens."

In vain did Hannah probe delicately to see if the Frenchwoman was at all interested romantically in the marquis. Yvonne would only say, rather primly, that she would always be grateful to Lord Ware, but showed no signs of any warmth at the mention of his name.

Hannah went back to her own room. She decided to wash her hair. Sir George would never see it, but with luck, Mrs. Clarence might, if Hannah could find her. She rang the bell and asked for extra cans of hot water and soft soap and then got to work, diligently drying her hair with a towel when she had finished and then rolling it in curl-papers.

Sleep did not come easily that night. She tossed and turned, occasionally dropping off into a fitful sleep, tormented by dreams of Sir George.

She woke in the morning, heavy-eyed, took out the curl-papers and brushed out her hair, too tired and depressed to admire the glossy result.

It was a sad party who climbed aboard the carriage. Benjamin took one look at his mistress's sad face and his conscience smote him afresh; the marquis was silent and withdrawn; and Yvonne looked heavy-eyed, as if she had enjoyed as little sleep as Hannah.

The weather was still fine. The splendid sight of the towers of York Minster rising above the fields did little to allay the gloom in the carriage. I should say something, the marquis was thinking. I should make some arrangement to call on her or I may never see her again. But he turned his mind to the immediate problem of her safety. He put his head out of the window and directed the coachman to take them to a posting-house near the Minster, at the centre of the town.

"No use in racking up at a coaching-inn," he said, sitting down. "Petit and Ashton will be watching all arrivals."

Soon the coach was rumbling over the cobbles of the twisting streets of York, the sun hidden above the overhanging medieval buildings.

The marquis noticed that Yvonne had taken some sort of map out of her reticule and was studying it closely. "I repeat my offer," he said gently. "You should not go alone."

She folded up the map quickly and put it back in her reticule. "I will do very well," she said, turning her face away but not before the watching Hannah had seen the glint of tears in her eyes.

The carriage rolled in under the arch of a posting-house called the Pelican and the passengers alighted. It had been a short journey that morning to York, but what with all the miles they had travelled from London, they felt shaky and wobbly like passengers alighting from a ship. It was as if their brief stay at Hadley Hall had never taken place.

Yvonne collected her small serviceable trunk and asked the marquis if she could leave it at the inn until she sent for it. Then she stood irresolute before holding out her hand to Hannah. "Goodbye, Miss Pym," she said. "I shall not forget you."

She curtsied to the marquis and then turned away. They stood helplessly, watching her slight figure disappear into the darkness of the arch and then out into a shaft of sunlight striking down between the buildings on the street. And then she was gone.

"What now?" asked Hannah bleakly.

"I will follow her," said the marquis. "Order rooms in my name, Miss Pym, and keep Miss Grenier's luggage with your own." He moved off quickly.

He stood outside in the street, looking to right and left, and was just in time to see Yvonne turning down a narrow street some distance away, holding that map in her hand. He ran lightly after her. Once she turned and looked back and he darted quickly into a doorway, and then, when she had continued her journey, followed her again.

A thin veil of cloud was beginning to cover the sun and he felt a dampness against his cheek that told him that rain was coming. On Yvonne walked, and on the marquis followed. She was approaching the outskirts of the town. People and houses were becoming fewer and he hoped she would not look back again.

And then she stopped. He drew back into the shadow of a small church. She was looking up at a shop and consulting her map. She went into the shop. The marquis waited a little. Yvonne came out of the shop and disappeared into a doorway next door to it.

The marquis left the church porch and hurried up to the building. At street level was a greengrocer's. Beside the shop was a doorway, obviously leading to flats above the shop. He tentatively pushed open the door in time to hear a scream of dismay. He darted up the stairs.

Yvonne was standing at the open door of a flat on the first floor, her hands to her mouth, staring in. He joined her.

He found himself looking into a living-room-cum-bedroom which had been well and truly ransacked. Papers were strewn everywhere, books had been tumbled from shelves, drawers ripped open, and the gutted mattress lay crazily, half off the bed, stuffing spilling out on the floor.

"Your father?" asked the marquis.

She gave a scream and jumped and then her fear died as she saw who it was.

"Gone," she said. "They must have found him."

He stepped past her into the room and stood looking at the debris.

"Whoever did this was looking for something," he said. "They may not have got Monsieur Grenier. Your father may have escaped them. Wait here. I'll ask that greengrocer."

He went downstairs and out into the street again and then into the fruit-and-vegetable-smelling darkness of the greengrocer's. The greengrocer, who appeared to be covered in as much earth as his potatoes, came shuffling forward. "What can I do for your honour?" he said, his little eyes taking in the richness of the marquis's clothes.

"The gentleman who lived in the room above the shop?" demanded the marquis.

"The Frenchie? Dunno. Ain't he above, Guv'ner?"

"No, he is not, and his room has been ransacked. Did you see anyone?"

"Not a soul, nor heard nothing either. I don't live over the shop. Got a place a bit away. Mr. Grenny that would be. Quiet gennelman, sir. No trouble. Pays reg'lar. Best get the parish constable."

The marquis went back to Yvonne, who was automatically trying to straighten things. "They must have taken him," she said desperately as soon as she saw the marquis. "His clothes are here."

"His razor?" asked the marquis. "His wallet? Personal papers?"

Yvonne searched thoroughly and then said with a rising note of hope in her voice, "His razor is gone and his toilet-case. Also, a miniature of Mama." Her face fell. "But this could be the burglary, non?"

"Burglars would not have left clothes behind, nor would they have rifled his papers. If your father escaped Petit, then why were they so interested in his papers?"

"Perhaps they were looking for his escape routes from France," said Yvonne.

"Perhaps." The marquis turned as the parish constable entered the room. He was a large bull-necked man with an expression of bovine stupidity. Yvonne was suddenly glad the marquis was with her. The fact that she and her missing father were both French made the constable suspicious from the outset. But to Yvonne's surprise, the marquis reported it as a burglary and possible assault. He made no mention of either Monsieur Petit or Mr. Ashton. Yvonne let him do all the talking while the policeman promised to report the matter to the authorities but managed to convey he intended to do nothing about it. Unlike France, Britain did not have a regular police force. Locals took turns at being parish constable, and most did as little as possible to enforce law and order during their spell of duty.

When they were alone again, Yvonne demanded, "Why did you not tell them of Petit?"

"To start talking about French spies to that thickhead would not get us anywhere, and Petit, if found by the authorities, might blacken your father's name. We must search for your father ourselves . . . if he is still at liberty. I shall search for Petit. If I find him, and he has not your father with him, then that means your father did escape."

She looked at him helplessly. "I don't know what to do."

He put his arms around her and drew her close. For a moment, she leaned against him and he could hear the beating of her heart. "I will take care of you," he said huskily.

She pulled free, her face flaming. "I am quite well able to take care of myself," she said tearfully, "without stooping to become some English aristocrat's kept creature!"

He had meant it as a proposal of marriage, he realized in a dazed way, but she was looking at him with such disgust mixed with fury that he found his temper rising. Be damned to her!

"I merely meant that I will fund your keep in York if you have not sufficient money," he said icily. "Then, when your father is found, he may repay me if he wishes."

"Oh, I am sorry," she said weakly. "Of course, I am grateful to you. You see," she said timidly, looking up into his bleak eyes, "in the households where I work I am in the way of being propositioned."

This had the effect of making him angrier than ever as a sharp stab of jealousy shot through him. But he forced himself to say quietly, "I will now escort you back to the inn.

The policeman knows where to find us if he wants us. You will feel better once you have seen Miss Pym again. Was the door of the room standing open?"

"No, I got the key from the greengrocer's." She held it out. He took it and locked the door securely.

When he returned the key to the greengrocer after telling Yvonne to wait for him outside the shop, he asked the man, "Is this a spare key? Would Mr. Grenier have the other?"

"No, your honour, the key's right there with t'others on a nail on the wall by the door."

"Not very safe, is it?" commented the marquis. "Anyone could help themselves."

"I'm here in the shop from six in the morning till late. Mr. Grenny, he says to leave the key there 'cos it's a big one to carry around and the other rooms are empty."

"Did anyone ask about the keys? Any visitors?"

The greengrocer wrinkled his earth-smeared brow. "Well, blessed if I ain't forgotten. It was a young chap, dressed very grand, come in one evening late and starts chatting and I was getting angry 'cos he wasn't buying nothing. Kept poking about with his cane. He points to the keys and says, 'what's them for?' Told him for the rooms above and which ones were for what door but that there ain't no one up there but a foreign gennelman. He goes away but then I sees him talking to an older man outside. Next thing, the older man comes in with the younger and the older one starts talking about the weather and I don't know what. Next thing, Mrs. Battersby down the road comes in for leeks and after I'd served her, the fine gents is gone. Demme if they didn't come back as I was putting up the shutters and the old one says as how he would like oranges. So I went to serve him, like."

"So they probably took the key, ransacked the room, and put it back."

"Why would I expect sech a thing to happen?" said the

greengrocer defensively. "Folks around here is law-abiding. I shouldn't ha' let to a foreigner in the first place."

"It was not the foreigner's fault, was it? Here, I will leave you a note for Mr. Grenier. Should he return, he will know where to find me. Until then, keep that key somewhere safe, and should those two gentlemen come back, let me know." The marquis took out one of his cards and scribbled the name of the Pelican on the back of it. Then he produced a notepad and wrote a short note to Monsieur Grenier, telling him that his daughter was at the inn.

He went out to join Yvonne. "Things are looking better," he said as they walked along the road. He told her of the visit to the greengrocer's of what had obviously been Ashton and Petit. "Had your father been there, there would have been some sort of a struggle," he said. "The greengrocer would have heard something. There is no back way out of that building that I can see."

A thin soft rain was falling. "No hacks in this district," he said, looking about. "Your pretty bonnet will be ruined."

"I am beyond worrying about clothes," sighed Yvonne as he hurried her along.

They walked in silence back the way they had come.

Hannah and Benjamin were in the coffee-room and both looked startled to see Yvonne. Quickly the marquis explained what had happened.

Benjamin's eyes lit up. Here was a way to make himself useful. "I'll start right away, my lord," he said eagerly. "They're bound to be at some inn in the city."

"See what you can do," said the marquis. "I think we should dine, Miss Pym—that is, if you have not already eaten?"

Hannah shook her head.

Yvonne leaned back in a chair, her eyes closed as the marquis ordered food to be served to them in a private parlour, her mind dimly registering again that the marquis did not seem to be impoverished in the slightest.

Benjamin went straight to the Bull, hoping to find Monsieur Petit and his friend Ashton, but not only were they not there but never had been. He trudged on around several more coaching-inns without success until it occurred to him that such as Petit, who could afford to hire a post-chaise from Grantham, might be found at a posting-house.

But at posting-house after posting-house he met the same reply. No one called Smith answering to the description of Petit and no one called Ashton either.

The earlier drizzle had changed to a steady downpour and Benjamin was weary and wet when he turned in at the welcoming door of a tavern on the outskirts of the town. He had already decided he did not like York. So many old buildings. So many wood-and-wattle houses. London was much more modern, thought Benjamin, forgetting that the Great Fire had done much to get rid of a vast number of antique buildings in the capital.

After taking off his wet coat and hanging it up to dry and shaking the raindrops from his beaver hat, Benjamin approached the cubby-hole of a bar and asked the pretty girl behind it to fetch him a tankard of shrub. While she was getting it, he turned around and surveyed the low-raftered, smoky room. A fire had just been lit in the grate, and fat raindrops dropped clear down the old chimney and hissed on the flames. Two men were seated by the fire, conversing in low voices. Benjamin turned back and was just about to pass the time in a little gentle dalliance with the serving maid when he distinctly heard one of the men at the fire curse in French. He recognized it as French, for he had heard Monsieur Petit use the same word when the marquis had chided him on his bad language. So he picked up his tankard and ambled over to the fireplace and said cheerfully, "Any room for me? The fine weather has broken and I confess to being chilled."

The two men were seated at a small table in front of the fire. They reluctantly made way for him, but glancing pointedly at all the other empty seats in the room.

They continued to converse in low voices, but in English.

"Really nasty weather," volunteered Benjamin cheerfully, wondering if he had imagined that French oath.

"Yes, very," agreed one of the men, and Benjamin brightened at the sound of the heavily accented English.

"Are you French?" he asked.

"Yes," came the reluctant reply.

"Must introduce myself. Benjamin Chubb, footman." Benjamin held out his hand. First one and then the other shook it.

"Our names are Chevenix and Deville," said Monsieur Deville.

"Honoured. I see your glasses are empty. What'll it be, gentlemen?"

"Well . . ." The two Frenchmen looked gratified, not being used to friendly treatment from Englishmen; despite the fact that there were thousands of French emigrés now resident in England, Messieurs Deville and Chevenix were used to being looked on with surly suspicion.

"Yes, of course you will," said Benjamin, getting to his feet. "What you having, then?"

"Claret, if you please."

Benjamin called over to the serving girl, who brought a jug of claret and three glasses.

"Now," said Benjamin, pouring wine for them, but deciding his own tankard of shrub was more to his taste, "confusion to Napoleon." The Frenchmen gravely drank the toast.

"In London," said Benjamin, "lot of you people live in the one quarter. I mean like in Cavendish Square and over in Sommers Town. Would there be a sort of French quarter in York?"

"Not really a quarter," said Monsieur Deville. "We all live in one narrow street, not a very romantic name, Bucket Lane."

"You wouldn't happen to have seen a tall Frenchman recently—white hair, pale eyes, yellar teeth, goes by the name of Monsieur Petit?"

Monsieur Deville shook his head. "A very common name. What does he do?"

Benjamin wrinkled his brow, thinking of what Yvonne had said. "Works in Paris, some sort o' judge on a tribunal."

Both men shot to their feet. Monsieur Chevenix was trembling. "Jacques Petit . . . *here*," he whispered.

"Sit down, sit down," begged Benjamin. "I ain't no friend o' his. Fact is, he's after someone my mistress wants to help. Sit down. I'll tell you."

Both men sat down gingerly, looking at Benjamin warily. He told them as much as he knew—how Yvonne had gone in search of her father, only to find him gone and his room rifled.

"So you see," ended Benjamin urgently, "maybe this Petit has got hold of Grenier. So I've got to find him."

"We both know Claude Grenier," said Monsieur Deville after a long silence. "He left our street a couple of months ago. He did say he was expecting his daughter, but that someone had got a message to him saying his life might be in danger, so he decided to move away from us other French people where he might feel safer. I am afraid that is all we know. But Monsieur Petit cannot openly come among us, for we would kill him. Where he can be, I do not know."

Benjamin finished his tankard of shrub, thanked them and left. Outside, the rain had stopped falling and a gusty wind was blowing shreds of paper and straw up to the overhanging eaves of the old houses.

He stood under the flickering light of a parish lamp and took a cheroot out from a case in his pocket and after much fumbling with a tinder-box managed to light it. He did not dare smoke in front of Hannah, who was even more stern in her admonitions against smoking than King James the First had been.

Where, oh where could he find Ashton and Petit? He did not want to return to Hannah with so little news. Ashton! He had forgotten that Ashton might have been the one to choose a place to stay. And what would a fop like Ashton do, who scrounged and primped and preened? Why, he would try to get them accepted as house guests in some comfortable household. But which one and where?

The livery stables, he thought suddenly. They might have hired some sort of carriage or gig. His quarry would not continue to use a post-chaise for town visits. He walked back towards the centre of town and asked where he might find the largest livery stable and was directed to a mews near the Minster. Big livery stables, as Benjamin knew, hardly ever closed down for the night, York being a main centre on the road down from Scotland. An ostler told him he was lucky. Mr. Peartree, who owned the stables, was working late in his office.

Mr. Peartree was bent over his ledgers, a small wizened man who smelled strongly of horse. He nonetheless considered himself a cut above speaking to servants and only treated Benjamin civilly because Benjamin was no ordinary servant but a liveried footman and might have a powerful master.

Benjamin knew that the name of Hannah Pym would carry little weight and claimed the Marquis of Ware as his master. He wondered, said Benjamin, whether two gentlemen had called a short time ago to hire some sort of carriage. He gave a rapid and unflattering description of both Ashton and Petit.

He waited anxiously while Mr. Peartree explored his wig meditatively with his quill-pen. Then Mr. Peartree said, "I bring 'em to mind now. Old feller didn't say much but the young one was all airs and graces and wanting a curricle at gig prices. What was it he said? 'We are going to Lord Wetherby's at Bradfield Park.' I says I didn't care where they was going, I wasn't letting my best curricle and horses out at cheap rates. So he paid up and the curricle came back all right, for they took one of my coachmen. Had he been going to drive it himself, I wouldn't have let it go, not for any money, for he had a shifty look. When coachee told me he had dropped them at Bradfield Park, I confess I was surprised, them not looking like the type Lord Wetherby would entertain."

Benjamin thanked him and strode back towards the Pelican. He felt he had been out all night, but the Minster clock boomed out ten strokes.

He found Hannah and Yvonne sitting in the private parlour, sewing. Hannah was neatly darning a hole in a stocking heel and Yvonne was adding a flounce to the hem of a gown.

Benjamin told them of what he had learned and Hannah's eyes flashed green. "Find Lord Ware," urged Hannah. "He will know what to do."

The marquis proved to be gone from the inn, and so they waited anxiously for his return.

It was nearly midnight when he came back. He listened carefully to Benjamin's story and then said, "You have had more success than I. But I do have a little news. I went back to the greengrocer's and hid in a doorway opposite and watched the shop. Ashton arrived and went in. The greengrocer saw him and started shouting, "Murderer!" at the top of his voice, and Ashton took to his heels and fled. I ran after him but he managed to lose me. It might mean he wanted to have a look through those papers again."

"So what do we do now?" asked Hannah. "Shall we go to the authorities and tell them what we know?"

The marquis paced up and down. "There is a slim chance they may have Monsieur Grenier under lock and key. If we have them arrested, we may never find him. Let me think. Wetherby. Thin, taciturn fellow, fat wife and, ah, a daughter of marriageable age." He suddenly smiled. "We shall call on Wetherby tomorrow."

"But you forget," protested Hannah, "Petit and Ashton will be in residence."

"And what can they say or do to us? Let us confront the enemy and keep a watch on him."

"But you are putting Miss Grenier at risk!"

The marquis's eyes rested on Yvonne. "I think not. We will make sure she is never alone. Now we should all go to bed so we shall be fresh for our adventures in the morning. More adventures for you, Miss Pym."

And no one to tell them to, thought Hannah suddenly, thinking of her lost love. Yvonne saw the sad look on Hannah's face.

As they were leaving the parlour, Yvonne put a timid hand on the marquis's sleeve and said quietly, "A word with you in private, milord."

Hannah looked back anxiously but Yvonne called, "I will be with you shortly."

The marquis leaned his broad shoulders against the panelled wall and smiled down at her in a way that made her feel weak. "What is it, Miss Grenier?"

"It is about Mees . . . Miss Pym."

"You disappoint me. Go ahead. What about Miss Pym?"

"If you remember the gossip about Miss Pym and Sir George?"

He nodded.

"Could you please, would you please, call on Sir George on your return to London and make sure he knows how distressed she is about the rumour? About how she fears she has lost his friendship?"

"For you, Miss Grenier," he said lightly and mockingly, "anything in the world."

She threw her head back. "Miss Pym is sad and worried. I owe her much. Do not take this request as a jest."

He straightened up and raised her hand to his lips and deposited a fleeting kiss on the back of it. "Be assured, I will do all in my power to secure Miss Pym's happiness."

Yvonne slowly withdrew her hand and dropped him a low curtsy. She had to pass very close to him to leave the room and she was intensely aware of him and of her own wicked hopes that he would pull her to him and kiss her.

But he made no move and so, with a breathless little "Good night," she went to see Hannah.

Hannah looked at her curiously as she entered the room. "What was all that about?" she asked.

"Just a personal matter," said Yvonne. "This business of calling on Lord Wetherby worries me. I do not think Lord Ware knows him very well at all. What do the aristocracy do if they do not want unwelcome guests?"

Hannah laughed. "They cannot really do much provided the unwanted guest is titled. They can pretend to be out, but that is difficult unless they have seen the arrival of the guests and warned the servants. Or they can say they are just leaving on a visit. I should think an acquaintanceship with the Marquis of Ware might hold a certain amount of social distinction, and as the marquis himself pointed out, they do have a marriageable daughter."

A shadow crossed Yvonne's face and Hannah wondered whether it was because she was thinking of meeting Monsieur Petit again or whether she was wondering about the marquis and that marriageable daughter.

"You had better get some sleep," she said gently. "Things will not seem so bad in the morning. I am sure you will see your father again soon. Just think! A resourceful gentleman like your father who arranged escapes out of France will know how to survive."

Yvonne gave Hannah an impulsive hug and then went off to her own room.

Hannah stirred up the coals in the fire. There were so many things she should have asked the marquis. Did he plan to confront Petit as soon as he got there? Did he plan to warn Lord Wetherby about the nature of the guests under his roof? She felt unusually weary. Usually before going to sleep, she read a chapter of the Bible, and then she would think about Sir George, would rehearse her stories, dreaming of seeing his sparkling blue eyes. But to think of him at all now gave her such an aching feeling of loss. How furious he must be with her!

It was two in the morning in London as Sir George Clarence walked slowly back from his club. In his pocket was Benjamin's letter. His first reaction on reading it had been disgust and distaste. But being a meticulous and fastidious man who knew that the target of any piece of gossip is usually the last to know, he had set out for his club with the express purpose of finding out what was being said.

He had, he realized at first, called at a bad time to find out anything, for all the gamblers, which meant, as far as he could see, all the present members of White's, were engrossed in gaming. He watched the play, waiting to see if some society gossip would give up and drop out, but it was not until after midnight when his patience was rewarded. Sir Paul Disley, a foppish and waspish baronet, rose from the table in disgust. Sir George waylaid him. "What about joining me in a bottle of port, Disley?"

"As long as it goes on your bill," said the baronet. "Deuced bunch of card sharks. I swear the cards are marked. Did ever a fellow have such monumental bad luck!"

Soon they were settled with a bottle of port between them. For the first time, Sir Paul seemed to realize the identity of his host. Sir George usually shunned types such as the fops and fribbles of society and was therefore damned as a "dry old stick." Sir Paul reflected that the company of such as Sir George Clarence was a fitting end to a disastrous evening.

"What have you been doin' with yourself?" he asked Sir George languidly and then his eyes sharpened as he remembered that delicious piece of gossip he had heard about the old diplomat.

Sir George leaned back in his chair. "I am here to find out about a certain rumour which has been circulating society about me and a certain lady."

Sir Paul looked as uncomfortable as if his companion had just been able to read his thoughts. "Lots of rumours," he said evasively. "Pay 'em no heed. I never do."

"Ah, but you see, the lady is not in town to defend herself. Pray tell me what you have heard."

Sir Paul wriggled in his chair and his eyes roved around the room looking for help. He had never come across a situation like this before and felt Sir George was behaving in a highly indecent manner. Everyone knew you talked about people *behind* their backs. It was flying in the face of good ton to ask them direct—or so went his rather incoherent thoughts.

"Oh, well, don't you know," he said helplessly.

"No, I do not know." Sir George's voice was clear and incisive. "I am waiting for you to tell me."

Sir Paul leaned forward. "They're saying as how you've got a certain Miss Pym in keeping, and that she used to be your brother's housekeeper."

"Ah," Sir George leaned back in his chair. Behind him in the other room, a game of hazard had just broken up and the players were beginning to filter through to the room in which he was sitting with Sir Paul. He raised his voice. "My dear Sir Paul," he said in carrying tones, "by coincidence my late brother had a housekeeper called Pym. I have a friend, a Miss Pym who is a distant relative of Mrs. Clarence, my sister-in-law. She is a gentlewoman of refinement and delicacy. I am going to seek out anyone who spreads libel and slander on Miss Pym's good name and take that person to court!"

There is nothing that strikes more terror into the upper-class soul than the thought of being dragged to court and accused of libel.

"I said nothing," squeaked Sir Paul.

"I am sure you did not," said Sir George smoothly. "But do put it about that I am out for revenge."

Now as he walked home, he was not so much angry any more at the insult to his name as concerned about Hannah. Damn that mischievous footman. What had he ever done to prompt that cheeky servant into thinking his feelings towards Miss Pym were more than that of a friend?

But he remembered the presents he had given her and he remembered with warmth the enjoyment and amusement her tales and adventures afforded him. She would know of the scandal and be feeling ashamed and distressed, and that he suddenly could not bear.

York, he thought, was so very far away. But not by mail-coach. It was a long journey by stage-coach, but the mails travelled as far as Edinburgh in only thirty-four and a half hours.

The gossip had sickened him of London society. He was a tired old retired diplomat who had not had any adventures in a long time. Would it be so very wrong to travel quickly to York and surprise Miss Pym?

He imagined the way those odd eyes of hers would light up.

He would do it! He would take the mail-coach in the morning, and check at each change of horses whether she was on any of the down coaches. He would feel rather silly travelling so far just to miss her.

Having come to this momentous decision, he felt younger than he had felt in years.

6

'Tis true, your budding Miss is very charming,
But shy and awkward at first coming out,
So much alarmed, that she is quite alarming,
All Giggle, Blush; half Pertness and half Pout.

—Lord Byron

As the adventurers travelled to Bradfield Park, a procession was making its way through York for the opening of the assizes. In front marched the judges in their huge powdered wigs and black gowns, then came the mayor and corporation, and then behind them footmen, liveried in white, with large nosegays in their buttonholes. The whole town was in motion, the streets full of young misses in white muslin, men in dark-blue coats and carefully brushed hats, and military people in red. There was an air of festivity and holiday.

Benjamin said that there were eight cases of murder to be tried at the assizes, among them a young couple charged with beating their own child to death. It seemed an odd occasion for holiday; English people priding themselves as they did on their humanity. The marquis said sourly that there usually was little else to watch in a country town.

For her part, Yvonne thought it odd to look out at this

parade of British justice and yet feel herself beyond the help of the law. As if he had been thinking the same thing, the marquis said, "We should really be going to Bradfield Park with a squad of militia to arrest Petit and Ashton, were it not for our concern for Monsieur Grenier."

The usually resolute Miss Pym was also feeling the chafing bonds of discretion. "Surely Monsieur Grenier would be safer if Petit and Ashton were arrested."

"They may yet have Grenier," said the marquis, "and that we must find out. Petit will no doubt have all his papers in order, forged papers to show that he arrived in this country during the brief break in hostilities with France. 'Are you Monsieur Petit of the Paris Tribunal?' 'No,' he will reply and he will produce excellent references to prove he is a traveller in French silks from Lyon or something like that. Ashton will cry innocence. A suspicious government will send Petit back to France and Ashton will go free. We must have some proof."

"Cannot they be arrested and made to speak?" asked Yvonne.

"No, my dear," said the marquis with a smile. "We have brutal ways of killing, but we no longer torture. We certainly often put people in the pillory and they are lucky if they can still be found alive after being stoned by the mob, but no one stands near them in their torment to hear a confession. So we shall be polite and English and enjoy the comedy. We know Monsieur Petit to be a dangerous man and Ashton a paid and dangerous fool. They know, *we* know, and so we now have to wonder where Lord Wetherby fits into the scheme of things. It is quite amazing what the impoverished aristocracy will occasionally do for money. And yet I have never heard it said that Wetherby is short of money."

"But quite a number of the aristocracy sympathized with the Revolution," said Hannah.

"*Before* the Revolution, Miss Pym. Yes, some had their sons taught trades and also their daughters, and even the ones who did not believe in the idea of liberty, equality, and fraternity also taught their children trades, convinced that England, too, would soon have a revolution and they wanted to make sure their sons and daughters could earn their bread." His eyes sharpened. "What is your father's trade, Miss Grenier?"

"A lawyer. He is an advocate."

"And we practise Common Law in England, not Roman Law, so he could not find employment. Can he do anything else?"

"He said that there were too many lawyers in France and that in any case, the law, such as it was, had become a farce. He was a trained carpenter, also."

"Aha! We should have thought of that." The marquis looked at Benjamin. "When we are settled in Bradfield Park, *if* we are settled in Bradfield Park, then I feel you should use those sharp wits of yours, Benjamin, and return to the town and find out if Monsieur Grenier is employed as a carpenter. I am surprised he gave his own name to the greengrocer. Mayhap he might be trading under an English name. Look for a common English name.

Bradfield Park was just outside York, only half a mile from the old city gates. Yvonne felt increasingly nervous as they turned in at the lodge.

The house itself, when they reached it, proved to be modern. Built only about thirty years ago, it was of square design, with Palladian windows and a white portico. They were alighting from their carriage when the marquis called, "Wetherby!" A thin little man carrying a gun at his hip and with a dog at his heels was strolling across the park. He scowled when he saw them and then came forward with obvious reluctance, his beady eyes on the luggage which Benjamin was unstrapping from the back of the carriage.

"Oh, it's you, Ware," said Lord Wetherby, peering up at the marquis. "Can't put you up. No room, no room. Excellent inns in York. Rather stay there myself. We've got a rotten cook."

The door of the mansion opened and a short, plump lady in a gauze cap and a chintz morning gown came hurrying up to them. "Bless my soul, it *is* Ware. I looked out of the morning-room and I said to Drusilla, 'Dusty,' I says, 'I swear that's the Marquis of Ware, or my name's not Wetherby,' And Dusty, she says to me, 'Oh, Mama,' " Here Lady Wetherby's voice rose to an alarming falsetto. " 'It can't be! Oh, my poor ickle heart.' The sweet child, for she saw you at Almack's and quite *dotes* on you."

"I am delighted to meet you again," murmured the marquis, sweeping her a magnificent bow and scrape. "May I introduce my cousin, Miss Grenier, and a dear old friend of my family, Miss Pym?"

"Delighted! Delighted! Such a pleasure. I said to Wetherby his wits must be wandering to allow such a loose screw as Ashton bed and board, for no prospects there whatsoever and poor Dusty yawns whenever she do see him, which is as little as the pet can help, her being sensitive and more suited to real *gentlemen* than fribbles."

Lord Wetherby poked the barrel of his gun into the turf at his feet and said moodily, "No room."

"No *room!*" echoed his spouse, her plump little mouth hanging open in surprise. "No room! Why, bless my soul, Wetherby, if you ain't shot your own brains out by mistake." Lady Wetherby threw back her head and laughed. "Haw! Haw! Haw!" Hannah reflected she had seen such laughter *written,* but it was the first time she had actually ever heard anyone laugh like that.

"We have *mountains* of room," gushed the ebullient Lady Wetherby, "and you must stay with us forever and ever, amen. Haw! Haw! Haw! And won't Dusty be in high alt. Come along! Come along! A little nuncheon, I think. Don't growl, Wetherby. You sound like your dog. And change into your morning dress, do. Don't you dare sit down in top-boots. Come along!"

Like an animated chintz-covered sofa, she waddled in front of them, calling to the servants, "The Blue Room for Lord Ware, Red Room for Miss What's-it, the young one, and the Yellow for Miss . . ."

"Pym," said Hannah shortly so as not to risk hearing herself described to the servants as the old What's-it.

"We shall have a cold collation in half an hour, Ware. Ring the bell and someone will show you the dining-room. Has not the weather been most glorious except for yesterday's rain? You must get Dusty to show you the gardens. The pet does so *dote* on flowers, being a delicate blossom herself."

Yvonne kept close to Hannah as they mounted the curved staircase behind a bombazine-gowned housekeeper. "I fear Lord Wetherby does not want us," whispered Yvonne.

"But her ladyship most certainly does," murmured Hannah, "and I think she rules the roost."

To Yvonne's relief her room was near Hannah's, with a sitting-room in between. The maids were unpacking their trunks when the marquis appeared and dismissed the servants. "Do not unpack too much," he said to Yvonne. "My bedchamber is along the corridor. You sleep there tonight and I will sleep here."

Yvonne nodded, her eyes wide with fright.

"Do not look like that," he said quickly. "I am sure neither Petit nor Ashton will dare to make a move while we are all here."

"Perhaps Lord Wetherby is a conspirator," suggested Hannah, who had entered Yvonne's room in time to hear the exchange.

"I would think that highly unlikely," said the marquis. "With such a man, the motive would need to be money and he seems to have plenty of that."

He left them to change. Yvonne put on her sprigged

muslin, wishing she had something new and pretty to wear to give herself courage.

She and Hannah went downstairs to the dining-room. Ashton and Petit were already there. Monsieur Petit's pale eyes wore a veiled look.

"We meet again," said Mr. Ashton. He was wearing a tight coat with very long tails and a ridiculously high collar. His painted face was embellished with a black patch on one rouged cheek.

"Yes, what a surprise. You *and* Monsieur Petit." said Hannah.

"Don't know who you mean," said Mr. Ashton curtly. "This here's my friend Mr. Smith."

"As you will," snapped Hannah.

The marquis and Lord and Lady Wetherby entered the room. "Dusty'll be along in a minute," said Lady Wetherby. "Says she's prettifying herself, as if she needed any embellishment. Blessed are the lilies of the field, I always say. Miss . . . er . . . have you met Mr. Ashton and his friend, Mr. Smith?"

"Pym," said Hannah severely. "Yes, we all met on the road north."

"Now ain't that a coincidence!" said Lady Wetherby, clapping her lace-mittened hands. "Just like poor Dusty pining after Ware here and then he lands on the doorstep. You can see the hand of God everywhere. Oh, here's my pet."

A breathtaking vision of blonde curls, blue eyes, and dimples trotted into the room. She was wearing a delicate muslin gown with a pink sprig. Pink silk ribbons were threaded round the low neckline and pink silk ribbons between the deep flounces at the hem. On top of her glossy curls was a knot of pink silk roses. She curtsied low to the company, looking up at the marquis with a fond, doting look.

"Now we're all here, pray be seated," said Lady Wetherby. "You there next to Dusty, Ware, and Misses . . . umer . . . there."

Hannah found herself seated between Ashton and Petit.

Yvonne felt suddenly homesick for her own country-women. These Englishwomen could be so silly. Only look at the way Dusty—stupid name—was flirting shamelessly with Ware, and of course, he was enjoying it! And she used such a lot of baby talk, it was hard to understand what she was saying.

For all but Lady Wetherby, her daughter, and the marquis, it was an uncomfortable meal. Ashton, Petit, Hannah and Yvonne ate in stony silence, and Lord Wetherby glared round the table as if wishing them all in hell.

At last it was over. Dusty prettily asked if she could show the marquis the succession houses and the marquis said he could think of no happier way of passing a summer's day. Yvonne's heart felt like a stone. She wondered if he would kiss Dusty in that shattering way.

But her spirits rose a little when Hannah suggested that they take a walk in the grounds. "You see," said Hannah, "as soon as they were out of earshot, "if perhaps Lord Wetherby is in on the plot, your father might be here. We can look as if we are admiring the gardens and take a walk around the house and find out if there is somewhere where he might be hidden."

"If they had him, would they not have taken him off to France?" asked Yvonne, although she was feeling cheered at the idea of doing something.

"They may have to wait for news of a ship," said Hannah. "Let us begin. Benjamin has gone back to York to see if he can find a trace of your father."

Benjamin walked through the busy streets of York. He was homesick for London. He longed for a game of dice. But he still had a bad conscience about Miss Pym and Sir George, and so he began to call at first one carpenter's shop and then the other. He had reached his third call at a furniture manu-factory when all his good resolutions began to fade. Three of the workmen were in the long, wood-scented shed playing dice. It was more than flesh and blood could bear. In no time at all, he was crouched down with them on the sawdust-covered floor, rattling the dice, feeling the old excitement coursing through his veins. He won a handful of silver and rose to his feet just as the foreman strode into the shed and the men leaped back to their work.

"What's all this?" demanded the foreman, glaring about. Benjamin flicked sawdust from his livery with a fastid-ious hand. "I am here looking for a certain carpenter—calls himself Grenier."

"Never heard of 'im," said the foreman. "Off with you and stop keeping my men from their work."

Benjamin went off whistling. The day was fine and he craved another game. He made his way to a tavern and soon was rattling the dice again, winning gold this time, for the company was of the gentleman class. Gambling fever created a democracy. Aristocrat would play with beggar. When the game was over, he asked for the nearest carpenter's and made his way there. And so the rest of the day wore on, with Benjamin interposing his calls on carpenter's shops with gam-bling in taverns.

He learned there was a carpenter's shop on the outskirts of town on his road back to Bradfield Park and called there just as the owner was locking the doors. Patiently, he asked the usual question. The owner, a Mr. Griggs, said he had never come across a carpenter of the name Grenier or Miller. "Wouldn't be in the trade yourself?" he asked. "I was short-staffed today, what with some of them demanding a holiday for the assizes. What's the fascination in sitting in a dusty court hearing poor wretches being sentenced to the rope? It's beyond me."

Benjamin straightened his livery. "I am a footman," he

said haughtily, if a trifle tipsily, for he had drunk quite a number of tankards of ale during his visits to the taverns.

"And what's a footman doing looking for a carpenter?"

"This carpenter is a friend of the Marquis of Ware," lied Benjamin.

"If he's a friend of a marquis, what's he doing working as a carpenter?"

"He ain't no ordinary carpenter," said Benjamin. "He's one of those Frenchies."

"Oh, an immigrant! We had one of those. Good worker."

"Name?"

"Called himself Green."

Green . . . Grenier, thought Benjamin, his interest quickening.

"What became of him?"

Mr. Griggs patted the now locked doors rather like a man patting a horse and turned round. "Well, he was working at the lathe when two men came in. He looked none too pleased to see them."

"Tall man wiff white 'air?" exclaimed Benjamin, whose accent always became cockney when he forgot to control it. "An' a foppish, prancing young fool?"

"Sounds like 'em."

"So what happened?"

"They come up to him and began to talk. Mr. Green took off his apron, hitched his coat and hat down from a nail on the wall, and just walked off with them. I ran after him and said, 'Hey, you can't just stop work when you feels like it.' He says as how he's sorry but he's got to go."

"Maybe they held a gun on 'im," said Benjamin, half to himself.

"Not that I could see," said Mr. Griggs. "Here! What's all this about?"

"Too long a story," said Benjamin over his shoulder as he strode off. He felt uneasy. If Mr. Grenier had just walked off, just like that, could it be that he had really changed his mind and wanted to go back to France with them?

But he wouldn't have disappeared like that without having let his daughter know, thought Benjamin. And he had surely used his real name at the greengrocer's so that his daughter would be sure of finding him.

The sky was turning a pale green and a bat fluttered high above his head. Better get back quickly and report what he knew. He stepped out smartly, but as he came abreast of a tavern he could hear the merry sound of voices, the tinkle of glasses, and the rattle of dice.

His feet seemed to have a life of their own, separate from his brain and his conscience, both of which were telling him to get back to Bradfield Park as quickly as possible with his news.

He saw that the men playing dice were finely dressed. He edged towards their table, waited until one threw up his hands in disgust and walked away, and neatly slid into his place.

Time flowed past as Benjamin's fortunes rose and sank and rose again. It was past midnight when the company declared the game at an end and urged Benjamin to join them in several bottles of wine.

"Must get back to Bradfield Park," said Benjamin.

"What, old Wetherby's place? You won't get much from him. Proper old skinflint," said one.

"House seems pretty grand," commented Benjamin, his clever black eyes roaming from face to face.

"Lady Wetherby holds the purse-strings," said another. "Wetherby speculated on 'Change and lost his fortune. Has to ask her for every penny."

Benjamin made his way out into the fresh air, trying to clear his tipsy brain. Lady Wetherby cracked the whip because she had the money. Therefore, it followed that Wetherby might want money of his own and might be prepared to assist a traitor to get it.

He went along the winding road feeling muzzy and tired. He sat down by the side of the road and put his head in his hands. He shouldn't have drunk so much. The next moment, he was fast asleep.

Hannah, Yvonne, and the marquis were in the little sitting-room between the bedchambers. The marquis had called to move his night-things to Yvonne's room and had found both of them dressed, awake, and worried.

Benjamin had not returned, explained Hannah. The marquis said he would wait with them. He was not so worried about Benjamin's fate as Hannah was, thinking that any unsupervised servant had probably taken to the town's taverns. Benjamin was quick and clever but no servant could surely be expected to play detective for very long when the delights of the town lured him.

Yvonne was quiet, stitching away, adding an extra flounce to another muslin gown, Hannah having given her a gown to cannibalize. She was turning the events of the day over in her mind. She and Hannah had searched the grounds and the house and had not found any place where a man might be hidden. When they had gathered in the drawing-room that evening, Mr. Ashton and Monsieur Petit were absent, as was their host. Lady Wetherby blithely said her husband had had some business to attend to in the town. The marquis, on hearing this, became convinced that Lord Wetherby was in on the plot and was glad he had not confided in him.

But Dusty had been very much in evidence, thought Yvonne, and she had been winsome, she had been charming, and she had been totally sickening. How could the marquis bear that unending stream of baby talk, that vacuous blue stare? But he had flirted easily with Dusty and had appeared to enjoy her company immensely.

"I suppose he will marry her." Yvonne turned brick-red when she realized she had voiced this thought aloud.

The marquis's silvery eyes glinted at her in the lamplight. "Who will marry whom?"

"I was remembering something, that is all," said Yvonne, pricking her finger with her needle and uttering an exclamation of dismay.

"If you mean I will marry Dusty, no, I do not think so," said the marquis. "But it is important that Lady Wetherby thinks so. I was talking to one of the gamekeepers and he told me that it is Lady Wetherby who has the money, but that she is nonetheless notoriously clutch-fisted. It is only the thought of my title and fortune that has made her welcome us."

"So you do have a fortune, Mr. Giles?"

"Yes, Miss Grenier."

"Then why the alias?"

"A whim. I am a whimsical fellow. I confess I sometimes do silly and irrational things."

"Do you kiss females when the whim takes you?" Yvonne's voice was sharp and Hannah looked from one to the other.

"Oh, yes. But that has proved too dangerous a sport. Do you know, Miss Pym, that the last lady I kissed had her revenge on me?"

"How could I, my lord? But how did she get her revenge?"

"She stole my heart."

"Miss Dusty, I suppose," said Yvonne waspishly.

"Now you are being deliberately obtuse."

"If I may interrupt your banter," said Hannah, "I would like to remind you that my Benjamin has not yet returned and I am nearly out of my wits with worry."

"If we took some action, we should feel better," said the marquis. "Let us walk a little way past the lodge gates and we might meet him coming home."

Hannah was relieved at the prospect of any action whatsoever. Soon the three were making their way down the long drive. Yvonne gave a little shiver and looked back. "I feel as if the whole house is watching us," she whispered.

"Do you not think that they might try to kidnap Miss Grenier?" suggested Hannah nervously. "I feel we have made a grievous error in coming here."

"They would not dare. Besides, I am convinced Lady Wetherby knows nothing of it."

"Why are you going along with this adventure, my lord?" asked Hannah. "If you travelled north with the sole purpose of calling on a friend, will not he or she be waiting for you?"

The marquis hesitated. If only he could be sure about Yvonne. If he could be sure she was not playing a deep game, then he would call the authorities to have Petit and Ashton arrested and then let them prove their innocence in a court of law. But he could not bear the idea of Yvonne herself having to stand trial. In his very English way, the marquis had doubts about Yvonne simply because no other women had ever aroused his senses so much. He wanted to marry her were she innocent. He could not marry a traitor. Perhaps she was used to charming men. She could certainly play the coquette very easily.

"Give me another day and I will tell you," he said.

They opened the small gate at the side of the larger lodge gates and let themselves out into the road. A bright moon was shining through the black lace of the trees above, harlequinning their faces in chequered patterns of silver and black.

"Oh, where can that wretched footman of mine be?" mourned Hannah.

"Why, there, I think," answered the marquis in a voice suddenly tinged with amusement. A little down the road, they could see a figure sitting on a milestone.

"It cannot be Benjamin," protested Hannah. "Why should he fall asleep by the roadside when he was so nearly at Bradfield Park?"

They approached the sleeping figure. It was indeed Benjamin, head buried in his cravat, hat tilted down over his face, snoring heavily.

"Wake up this minute!" shouted Hannah, angry with relief.

Benjamin started awake, screamed, "Spies!" and fell over behind the milestone.

"Faugh! What a smell of beer." Hannah wrinkled her nose in disgust. "And tobacco. Get up, you lazy hound, and present yourself."

Benjamin, now fully awake and sobered, clambered out onto the road and said huffily, "I was exhausted, modom, what with trudging around all them carpenters."

"And taverns, by the smell of it." Hannah gave his arm an irritated shake. "Well, what did you find, if anything?"

So Benjamin told them of how Ashton and Petit had visited Grenier where he was working and how he had evidently gone off with them without a struggle.

"So if he went willingly, he is somewhere about in hiding," said the marquis. "If not, in captivity. We have played cat and mouse long enough. The time has come to confront Lord Wetherby with what we know."

"My father would never have gone willingly with them," exclaimed Yvonne.

The marquis's voice held a cold edge. "You have not seen him for some time. He may have changed."

"Never!"

"Let's not stand here arguing," pleaded Hannah. "We must go back to the house and try to find Lord Wetherby if he has returned."

They silently made their way back up and through the lodge gates and up the drive under the thicker blackness of the trees in the park. Then Yvonne let out an exclamation. "I am . . . how you say . . . tripping over my shoe-lace." They waited as she bent to tie it. And then, in the stillness of the night, the marquis distinctly heard a gun being cocked nearby.

"On your faces," he shouted. He put an arm round Hannah and an arm around Yvonne, who had just straightened up, and bore them face downwards on the grass beside the drive. "What . . . ?" began Benjamin, who was still standing. There was the sound of a report and a bullet whizzed through Benjamin's tall hat. He let out a screech and fell on his face on the grass.

"They've killed Benjamin," wailed Hannah, crawling on her hands and knees towards her footman's fallen body.

"No, modom," came Benjamin's voice, "but the bleeders 'ave wounded me dimmed 'at."

"Stay where you are," whispered the marquis. He sat up cautiously and drew a pistol from his pocket. Then, holding it primed and ready, he eased himself to his feet. A bullet whizzed past his ear and the marquis took aim and fired in the direction from which the shot had come. There was a sharp scream of pain, then the sound of breaking twigs and branches, then nothing.

"I think I wounded whoever it was," said the marquis in a low voice. "On your feet and let us make rapidly for the house."

Hannah found her mouth was dry with fear. She put an arm around Yvonne's waist and ran with her towards the shelter of the portico. The marquis and Benjamin soon joined them. They had waited behind, the marquis with his gun at the ready, until they were sure the two women were safe.

"Now," said the marquis. "Let's rouse this household."

In the hall, he rang the bell until the butler appeared in his night-shirt. The marquis ordered him to rouse the staff and then Lord and Lady Wetherby.

Lord Wetherby proved to be at home and came down the staircase with his wife, both of them looking very angry indeed.

"What is the meaning of this, Ware?" demanded Lady

Wetherby. "Is not my Dusty to get her beauty sleep? 'Stay in your room, pet,' that's what I told her, for ten to one they're all drunk."

"We went out to look for Miss Pym's missing footman," said the marquis, addressing both servants and master. "On the road back through the park and not far from the lodge gates, someone tried to kill us. Someone shot at us. As you are here, Lord Wetherby, I am sure our assailant was either Ashton or Petit—by the latter I mean the man who calls himself Smith. They are spies for the French, so what are you doing giving them house room?"

"I didn't know who they were," raged Lord Wetherby. "I mean,,I know that loose screw, Ashton. Why should I turn 'em away? Said they were only going to stay a few days. French spies be damned. You're romancing, that's what. Been at the brandy, hey?"

"You will soon be making a statement to the nearest magistrate," said the marquis, "for I intend to go to the authorities in the morning and put the whole case before them."

"You do that," shouted Wetherby. "And then take yourself off and those women with you."

Lady Wetherby looked alarmed. "Watch your tongue, Wetherby," she said, "and don't you go insulting Ware like that or you'll have our Dusty heart-broken. Don't she dote on Ware already? Don't he dote on her? Well, now."

She folded her surprisingly strong arms under her ample bosom.

"Dote on Dusty, dote on Dusty," shrieked Lord Wetherby, suddenly beside himself with rage. "Everything for bloody Dusty and nothing for me. Gowns that cost hundreds of pounds for Dusty, and if I want a new hunting dog, you won't loosen those purse-strings. Well, let me tell you this. If you think Ware cares a fig for dear little Dusty, you are a bigger cretin than I thought you were. His most noble lordship has only got eyes for that French *cousin* of his, and if you weren't so blind, you would see it."

"He can't marry his cousin," shouted Lady Wetherby. "Produce totty-headed brats if he marries his cousin, you old fool. Course I don't give you any money. You'd just lose it like you did your own."

"Enough of this," said the marquis. "Where are Petit and Ashton?"

"Beg pardon," said the butler, "but they aren't in their rooms and their luggage has gone."

The marquis gave an exclamation of disgust. "Now we may never find them." He turned to Hannah. "Take Miss Grenier to her room. She can sleep in her own room tonight." Lady Wetherby heard this, misinterpreted it, and let out an outraged squawk. The marquis ignored her.

"Come along," said Hannah gently. "A good night's sleep is what you need."

She led Yvonne up the stairs and then stayed with her until she was safely in bed before retiring herself. Hannah fell almost instantly into a dreamless sleep.

Yvonne awoke an hour later. Someone was shaking her gently by the shoulder. "Miss Pym," she exclaimed, sitting up in bed.

"No," said the voice she had come to hate and dread. "It is I, Petit. I have your father. If you want to see him alive, you had better get dressed and come quietly. One scream from you, and I will return to where he is hidden and kill him on the spot. If you come quietly, he will live to stand trial."

Yvonne climbed slowly down from the high bed. He lit a candle on the mantelshelf and she saw he held a gun. "Was that you, shooting at us in the park?" she whispered.

"No, that fool Ashton. One of you winged him, and serves him right. He thought he would take matters into his own hands and kill Ware and so make matters easier. He was hiding in the park, waiting for me when he heard you return. Get dressed!"

Numbly, Yvonne did as she was told, using the bedcurtains as a screen. Monsieur Petit dropped a letter on her pillow. It was addressed to Miss Pym and the Marquis of Ware. "That should keep them quiet," he said.

Seeing that Yvonne was ready, he held open the door for her and then closed in behind her with the gun at her back.

To die will be an awfully big adventure.

—Sir James Barrie

Sir George Clarence climbed down stiffly from the mail-coach outside the Bull. He stood in the sunlight of the inn yard and looked about him. The day was still and warm. He decided to reserve a room for himself at the inn before going in search of Miss Pym. Perhaps she might be resident at the inn herself. He had asked about her at all the stops on the road up, but there had been no news of any Miss Pym travelling in the opposite direction.

Inside the Bull, they told him that yes, he could have a room; but no, there was no Miss Pym.

Sir George followed his luggage upstairs, feeling slightly flat. He had somehow imagined that Miss Pym would be there, waiting for him.

He was also beginning to be plagued by a nagging doubt about Miss Pym's fantastic stories. Could she really have had so many amazing adventures? He himself had suffered a quiet but dull journey in the company of a highly respectable lawyer, his wife, and a Scottish lord of ancient years who took snuff for what seemed like the whole of the journey. But he had come to see her, and see her he would. He shaved and washed and changed and went down to the stage-coach booking office just to make sure that her name was not already down for the journey back; but again, there was no mention of Miss Pym.

After a good breakfast, he sallied forth in a light gig to call at the other hostelries in the town, drawing a blank at first one and then the other. He was just negotiating through the press of traffic outside the Minster when he let out an exclamation. He was sure he had just seen a familiar figure turning in at the door of the great cathedral.

After some difficulty, he found a place for his horse and gig, and then hurried off into the Minster.

He stood for a moment taken aback by the lightness and beauty of the interior, and then moved forward. All was calm and hushed and quiet. Great shafts of sunlight shone through the magnificent stained-glass windows, splashing patterns of colour across the nave.

And there, in the centre of the nave, stood that familiar slim figure. He found his heart was beating hard.

"Lucinda," he said softly. "Lucy. Is that you?"

She turned to face him, her eyes widening in surprise, and he found himself looking at his sister-in-law, Mrs. Clarence.

She was as beautiful as ever, although there were little lines etched around her eyes and mouth. She held out both hands to him, crying, "My dear George. Oh, my very dear George."

"Shhhh!" hissed a verger waspishly.

"Come outside," urged Sir George. "Let us find somewhere where we can talk."

Arm in arm, they walked to a pastry cook's near the Minster. "I will tell you why I am here when we are seated," said Sir George.

She was still graceful, still elegant, he thought in wonder, as she poured tea and smiled on him, her eyes sparkling with warmth.

"Your news first," said Sir George, picking up his old-fashioned handle-less teacup. "Do you know Jeffrey is dead?"

Her eyes clouded over. "Yes, I read the obituary in the newspaper."

"And are you still with . . . ?" He paused delicately.

"John. John Hughes. We are to be married next week, very quietly of course. You must blame me . . ."

"Not I," said Sir George stoutly. "You forget, my dear, I knew my brother very well, and he was always, even before his marriage to you, a moody and depressed man."

Mrs. Clarence looked wistful. "I thought before we were wed that his moodiness was a mixture of the lover and the poet."

"So how do you live, Lucy? What do you do?"

"I am a farmer's wife now. John did not want to live on my money, so we bought a tidy farm and he made it pay. Such work, such long hours."

"And children?"

Her fine eyes flashed. "Two," she said merrily. "Two little boys."

"And do you still have to work so very hard?"

"Oh, now I have no end of servants. John made the farm very prosperous. He paid me back all the money he had borrowed to buy the farm. We are very grand. But what of your news, George? I heard you had retired. And why are you in York?"

He leaned back in his chair and smiled. "Do you remember Hannah Pym?"

"My housekeeper! Of course!"

"Well, it is a long story but I will try to make it as brief as possible. My brother left Miss Pym five thousand pounds in his will. I took a fancy to Miss Pym. I remember the morning after the reading of the will, seeing her standing by the window at Thornton Hall watching the stage-coach going by. She said she wanted to travel—on the Flying Machines. And that was the start of her adventures."

He told Mrs. Clarence of some of Hannah's adventures while she laughed and exclaimed. When he had finished, she asked, "And is that what brings you to York? To find some adventures of your own?"

"No." He looked embarrassed. "The fact is that that footman of hers, Benjamin, the one I told you about, he ... well ... he decided that there might be a romance in the offing and so, I think, to prompt marriage or twist my arm in some way ... anyway, he told London's biggest gossip, Mrs. Courtney, that I was keeping my brother's ex-housekeeper as mistress. I scotched the rumour, I hope, by saying that the Miss Pym who was a friend of mine was not the housekeeper but someone from your side of the family. I also threatened to sue anyone who continued to talk libel. But I knew how very distressed Miss Pym must be. I came north on an impulse ... to find her, to explain that true friends never paid any heed to malicious gossip."

She gazed at him quizzically and he flushed a little and looked down. She opened her mouth to say something and then closed it again. She had been about to tease him but had decided against it. Hannah Pym. She remembered Hannah, the waif of a scullery maid who had risen up the ranks of the servants, indomitable Hannah with her square shoulders, odd eyes, and fierce loyalty. Instead she said, "And have you found her?"

"I only arrived this morning, but so far have not been able to locate her."

"Where have you tried?"

He took out a notebook and began to reel off the names of the main coaching-inns.

"Miss Pym appears to gravitate to grand company on

her travels. It would do no harm to try the posting-houses, starting with the best."

"Which is?"

"The Pelican. Not far from here. I will come with you if you like. It is within walking distance."

They finished their tea and cakes and walked out into the sunlight together.

At the Pelican they were told to their delight that Miss Pym had been staying there but had left with the Marquis of Ware to go on a visit to Bradfield Park, home of Lord Wetherby.

"What did I tell you," said Mrs. Clarence with a surprisingly youthful giggle. "Miss Pym only moves in the *best* circles. I have my carriage. Stable your gig and come with me and meet my John, and then we will go together and surprise Miss Pym."

Sir George found he was nervous at the prospect of meeting this ex-footman who had run off with his sister-in-law, fearing he would prove to be a boorish peasant of a fellow.

Rosewood Farm, Mrs. Clarence's home, turned out to be a fine building set among prosperous-looking fields. John Hughes was standing in the farmyard talking to some of the men when they drove up. He led them into the house and said he would change and join them presently.

Sir George was ushered into a sunny parlour. Mrs. Clarence had not lost her touch, he noted. The furnishings were in exquisite taste; the latest in light and delicate chairs and tables, and great bowls of roses to scent the air. He complimented her on her home. "Thank you," she said. "It was not like this when we first came here. Such a lot of work was needed to put it in good order. Oh, here is John." And what a world of love was in her eyes, marvelled Sir George, as she turned her face up to her husband.

He was a tall, well-built, quiet man, very shy but courteous. Sir George asked him about the farm and John grew animated as he described the improvements he had made and the bumper harvest he expected.

He then listened in amazement to the tale of Hannah Pym whom, he said ruefully, he remembered as a Tartar. "So will you come to Bradfield Park with us, John?" asked Mrs. Clarence.

He shook his head. "I must get changed and get back out in the fields again. You go, Lucy, with Sir George, and see if you can bring Miss Pym back with you this evening."

As Sir George and Mrs. Clarence drove towards Bradfield Park, Sir George said uneasily, "Do you think all Miss Pym's stories can be true? I had a dreadfully dull journey, no fair maids, no highwaymen."

"Oh, I am sure they are." Mrs. Clarence gave a gurgle of laughter. "I think there are people in the world like Miss Pym who make adventures happen. But she is staying at a highly respectable house, so I suppose she is finding it all rather dull after her recent hair-raising experiences and will be glad to see us!"

That morning, Hannah rose early and went through to Yvonne's room. For a moment she stood very still, looking at the empty bed and then seeing the letter on the pillow. Her first thought was that Yvonne had run away.

She opened the letter and read it and then turned white with shock. It was unsigned but she was left in no doubt as to whom it was from. "We have Miss Grenier," she read. "She has a chance to stay Alive and Stand Trial with Her Father in France. If you alert The Authorities, then I shall kill her before you can reach her."

Hannah stumbled along to the marquis's room. He was awake and dressed and just putting on his coat as she erupted into his room.

He silently read the letter, his face grim.

"Fools that we were," he said bitterly. "We should have brought in the militia to arrest them while we had the chance. Where can they have gone?"

"We will ask the servants if they have seen anything," said Hannah.

"We cannot do that. I think Petit would carry out the threat to kill her if we ask anyone for help. Rouse Benjamin. We will search the grounds and see if there is a clue to which way they went."

Benjamin, his head aching from his libations of the night before, joined them in front of the house. They stared this way and that in the bright sunlight.

"I do not know which way to go," mourned Hannah. "Oh, God, send us some sign."

"Look at that!" Benjamin's sharp eyes had seen something at the edge of the grass. He bent down and picked it up and then held it out to the marquis and Hannah. It was a small seed pearl.

"She was wearing a necklace of seed pearls," said Hannah excitedly. "She hardly ever took it off." They bent down and searched the grass. A few yards farther on across the lawn, they found another. They searched, sometimes thinking they had lost the trail, but then finding another, and another. And then the trail finally disappeared and they stood, wondering what to do.

"Listen!" The marquis held up his hand.

"Water," said Benjamin. "There's a river. Look, there's a little path over there."

The path twisted under overhanging trees, still muddy from the recent rain. The marquis silently pointed down at two sets of footprints in the mud, small footprints and large ones.

"Quietly now," he whispered. "They may be close."

In single file they edged along the path, which suddenly opened out into a small clearing at the water's edge. A stream flowed languidly past. Tied to a small wooden jetty at the edge of the river were three rowing-boats. "And see the other rope," said the marquis. "There was another boat here. Miss Pym, you wait here and I will go on with Benjamin."

"No," said Hannah firmly. "Miss Grenier is in peril. I am not going back."

In vain did the marquis remonstrate. Hannah stood firm.

Damning all pig-headed spinsters under his breath, the marquis gave in and helped Hannah aboard the rowing-boat while he took the oars. Benjamin crouched in the bow. "Now which way, I wonder?" said the marquis.

"There's something there, on a branch, downstream," cried Benjamin. "Something white. Row there!"

The marquis rowed to where he had pointed, the boat sliding easily downstream. Caught in a branch at a bend in the river, hanging from a sapling like a small brave flag, was a torn piece of sprig muslin. Benjamin snatched it and held it up triumphantly. "She kept 'er wits," he grinned. "Row on, me lord, and I'll look out for anything more."

Hannah, seated in the stern of the small boat, gazed about her with a sort of awe that both day and scenery should be so very beautiful.

Benjamin strained his eyes but could see no further markers left by Yvonne, but at least she had managed to leave that little bit of muslin to show them the direction in which she had been taken.

"There's some sort of building up ahead," called Benjamin. They slid towards it. It was a low square cottage with smoke rising from the chimney. A trim vegetable garden ran down to the river. A man was digging a row of cabbages.

The marquis rowed the boat into the soft mud at the riverbank and called to the man, who lumbered down slowly towards them.

"Seen any strangers about?" asked the marquis.

"Only yourselves," replied the man slowly.

"What lies further downstream? Is there another building?"

The man looked at the sky and looked at the ground until Hannah wondered desperately whether he had been struck dumb. At last he said ruminatively, "There be a bit of a hut. Used for fishing in his old lordship's time, folk do say."

"And how far on?" asked the marquis.

"Reckon about a mile."

The marquis thanked him and pushed the boat away from the bank and began to row again. Benjamin still looked for any sign left by Yvonne but could see nothing. The current was stronger now and helping the boat to race along. They came round another bend, much farther on, and there, among a stand of trees near the water's edge, stood the hut, and tied to a post on the bank was the other boat.

The marquis was about to ship the oars and let the boat glide into the bank, but Benjamin, elated at the sight of the hut, yelled, "Halloo, I'm sure we've found 'em!"

"Shut up, you fool!" hissed the marquis as the prow of the boat dug into the mud. He seized an oar to push off again, but he was too late.

The bushes on the river bank parted and there stood Ashton and Petit, with guns levelled on them.

Mr. Ashton was in his shirt-sleeves and had one arm bound up. He glared malevolently at the marquis. "Welcome," said Monsieur Petit, baring his yellow fangs in a smile. "Our guests will be delighted to have company. Get out of that boat with your hands above your heads and march towards the hut."

There was nothing else they could do but obey. The marquis was cursing himself. He had been so sure the night before that Petit and Ashton had fled.

Hannah wondered what would become of them all. She did not want to die. She suddenly most desperately did not want to die and leave Sir George Clarence with only the memory of one silly, romantical spinster.

"Inside," ordered Mr. Ashton when they reached the open door of the hut. Hannah, the first, went inside and stopped with an exclamation of dismay. Yvonne and what must surely be her father were lying on the floor, trussed up, gagged, and bound.

"Move forward," barked Mr. Ashton, a menacing figure now.

When he had them lined up inside, he held his gun to Yvonne's head so that they would submit docilely to being bound and gagged by Petit.

"Now," said Mr. Ashton with an evil grin, "we've got you just where we want you. We're going into town to get word of a boat that will take us to France. When we return, we'll take the Greniers with us and you three can stay here until you rot."

Monsieur Petit laughed. "Au revoir," he said, kissing his hand to them. The next thing, the door of the hut was slammed shut and they could hear a bolt being driven across the door.

The marquis looked at Yvonne. Large tears were rolling down her cheeks and he swore that if he ever got free of this predicament, he would cheerfully strangle both Petit and Ashton with his bare hands.

Mrs. Clarence and Sir George arrived at Bradfield Park and gave their cards to the butler. He returned after a short while to say gravely that my lord and lady were "not at home."

"But what of their guests?" exclaimed Mrs. Clarence. "The Marquis of Ware and Miss Pym?"

"I believe his lordship and his party went out early this morning," said the butler. "They have not returned."

Outside, Mrs. Clarence hesitated beside the carriage. "I can hear voices coming from the side of the house," she said. "It sounds like it might be the Wetherbys."

"Oh, I have no doubt they are at home," said Sir George. "It's just that they don't want to receive us."

"Let us just walk around towards the sound of their voices," urged Mrs. Clarence. "If we find them sitting in the garden, we can ask them if *they* know when Miss Pym and the others are due to return."

Together they walked around the corner of the house. There was no one in the garden, but the windows of a room overlooking the terrace were open and voices reached their ears clearly.

"But I'm sure he's in love with me, Papa," wailed a young female voice.

"The man's deranged," barked a masculine voice. Lord Wetherby, guessed the listeners. "Saying I've been keeping French spies in the house, saying they were shot at, threatening to call in the authorities. Never heard such rubbish. I tell you, Dusty, they were all foxed, including that crooked-nosed spinster."

"They must be coming back," said Dusty. "They haven't taken their luggage. Where did they go?"

"Do not take on so," came Lady Wetherby's voice. "Your father has the right of it. They are all mad. That Miss Pym, Ware, and that rude footman were seen walking doubled up across the lawn and then they got in a rowing-boat and sailed off downstream. I hope they drown. Poor pet. Mama shall find you a *proper* beau."

Sir George caught Mrs. Clarence by the arm and drew her back a little. "It is all very odd," he whispered. "Something is badly wrong here. I know Ware slightly and he is not the sort of man to make up stories about French spies. I would like to find him and ask him what is going on." He rubbed his brow and then made up his mind. "I think you had better return to your John while I go down the river and see if I can find them. I shall call on you this evening. If I do not call, I think you should get John to take this fantastical tale we have just overheard to the nearest barracks and tell the colonel to send some men to search down the river for us."

She nodded, wide-eyed. "Miss Pym is in the thick of an adventure after all," she said.

Sir George crossed the lawns towards the river, feeling conspicuous, wondering if Lord Wetherby might see him and send a gamekeeper after him to accuse him of trespass. He saw a glint of water in the distance through a gap in the trees and made his way there. With the sun shining down and the birds singing and the air full of the scent of roses, it was hard to believe in French spies or in anything bad at all.

He found the rowing-boats, noticing that two were missing, if the posts to which the boats were moored were any indication. He climbed gingerly into one of them, took off his coat and laid it carefully on one of the seats, untied the boat, sat down and picked up the oars. He would go downstream, and if he failed to find any sign of Miss Pym, he could always try to find some peasant who would be glad of some money for the job of rowing him back.

Although he was well aware the current was doing most of the work, he felt amazingly young and athletic as the boat slid easily down the river.

His enjoyment in the beauty of the day sharpened. He could not believe there was any danger. He would find Miss Pym and her companions picnicking beside the river bank. He imagined how Miss Pym's odd eyes would light up when she saw him. London with all its petty society gossip seemed far away.

A cottage came into view and he saw a man working in the vegetable garden and a woman getting water from a pump outside the house. He moored the boat and called to the man, who came very slowly to the water's edge and looked at him curiously.

"I am searching for the Marquis of Ware," said Sir George.

The man scratched his head with one earthy calloused

hand and stared up at the sky as if for inspiration. "Dunno," he said at last. "Try Bradfield Park."

"I *have* tried there. I was told the marquis and his party had gone out on the river."

The man stood as if turned to stone, his mouth hanging a little open. Sir George gave an impatient noise and lifted one of the oars to push off.

"Folks asking questions all day long," said the man suddenly. "Grand gennelman and a lady and footman went on down."

"Thank you," said Sir George, suddenly elated. "How far did they mean to go?"

Again that maddening silence, but this time Sir George waited.

"Asked about a building," said the man. "Told 'em about a fishing hut, 'bout a mile further down."

Sir George set off again. He was beginning to feel rather tired. It had been a long day and he had only slept fitfully in the mail-coach during the night. Unlike the stage-coaches, the mail-coaches kept going night as well as day.

Then he saw what must be the fishing hut, but his heart sank a little, for there was no sign of anyone about. But there was a rowing-boat tied up at the water's edge. They must be somewhere around.

He tied up his own boat alongside it and climbed rather stiffly up the bank, putting on his coat as he did so. The fishing hut stood in a clearing at the water's edge. Everything was very quiet and still, apart from the rushing of the water.

He began to feel uneasy and could not think why. The stillness of the place began to seem unnatural and he looked uneasily about him as he approached the fishing hut. The door was closed. There was a new shiny bolt across it. Well, they would hardly be bolted inside a fishing hut on such a glorious day. He would need to return to see if he could row against the current as far as that fellow at the cottage and ask there for help in getting back.

He half turned to go. And then he heard a noise from inside.

Hannah lay on the earthen floor in an agony of pain and misery. The ropes which bound her had been tied so tightly that she wondered—were she ever released—if she would be able to walk again.

The marquis was now lying still. He had been straining and wriggling in his bonds for the past two hours. In the gloomy light, Monsieur Grenier, a frail-looking man, lay as still as death. Hannah prayed he was still alive. She prayed for a lot of things apart from the well-being of Yvonne's father. She prayed for rescue. She prayed for life. She prayed the stinking gag in her mouth would not make her sick and tried to ignore the heavings of her stomach.

And in and out her tortured thoughts went the face of Sir George Clarence. If she did not return to London, he would assume she was too ashamed to show her face. A dry sob shook Hannah's thin body. In a book, he would ride to her rescue on a white charger and pull her up onto his saddle-bow. "And very silly and uncomfortable that would be," Hannah told herself sternly.

A wave of fury and despair at her own helplessness seized her and she banged her feet on the floor and strained at the cruel bonds that held her.

And then she heard the bolt being shot back. Hannah stiffened. She was sure that Petit would take the Greniers away and leave herself, Benjamin, and the marquis to rot, just as they had threatened to do.

She rolled over and faced the door. It opened very slowly and cautiously.

At first Hannah thought it was a vision—a vision of Sir George Clarence, standing in the sunlight and looking into the darkness of the hut.

And then his voice sounded in her ears. "My dear Miss Pym. This is terrible." And then he was kneeling beside her, fumbling in his pocket for his penknife. He sawed through her bonds and then removed her gag. Hannah let out a wail of pain and began to rub her wrists and ankles.

"Gently," he said. "Where are the men who did this?"

"Gone," croaked Hannah. "But they will soon be back. But how . . . ?"

"In a minute, my dear friend, let me attend to the others."

He set about cutting the others free, first Yvonne and then the rest. Yvonne crawled to her father's side, whispering in French, "Papa, are you all right?"

Monsieur Grenier's eyes fluttered open. "I will live," he said. "They gave me a nasty blow on the head when I tried to escape and then tied me up."

Sir George produced a small flask of brandy and held it to his lips. He drank a little and some colour came to his white cheeks. He was a small man, slight of stature, and with thick brown hair streaked with grey.

"Introduce us to our rescuer, Miss Pym," said the marquis.

"This," said Hannah proudly, "is Sir George Clarence."

"Of course it is," said the marquis. "But I could hardly expect to see you in the wilds of Yorkshire, Sir George. Before we have any further explanations, I think we should escape as quickly as possible, although I swear, were the ladies not with us, I would wait here for Petit and Ashton and tear them apart with my bare hands."

The next moment, Sir George realized why Miss Pym had so many adventures. She said, "Why do we not wait for them to return?"

"My dear Miss Pym," cried Yvonne. "They are armed and we are not. They took milord's pistol from him."

"I'll never walk again," shrieked Benjamin suddenly, as he tried to stand up. "I'll murder those bastard twats. I'll—"

"And I'll gag you again, you foul-mouthed servant," raged the marquis. "Never again let me hear you use such language in the presence of ladies."

"Rub your wrists and ankles hard, Benjamin," ordered Hannah. She looked at Sir George and the marquis. "You see, I had little else to do but think of revenge. We could hide in the woods at the back and wait for them to return. When they walk inside the hut, we shall simply bolt the door on them."

"And do you think, Miss Pym, that they are going to stroll into an empty hut?" demanded the marquis testily.

"We could perhaps make dummies of ourselves and leave them lying on the floor with some of our clothes on them," said Hannah eagerly. "Then, when Ashton and Petit are inside stooped over the dummies, we can slam and bolt the door and we have them!"

"But," said Sir George patiently, "all they have to do is shoot the bolt off the door. They will be armed, you know."

Hannah looked disappointed.

"And even if we succeeded," said the marquis, obviously restraining himself from shouting at Hannah to take Yvonne away to safety, "may I remind you of the risks. Furthermore, to subject Miss Grenier and her poor father to any more danger would be folly."

Monsieur Grenier found his voice. "If there were any way of capturing them," he said in good English, "then I would be prepared to help you, Miss Pym. I am not so weak as I look. They did feed me. I was being kept in prime condition for my trial."

Benjamin, who had slipped outside during this exchange, came dancing back. "There's fallen trees, stacked ready to be chopped at the back," he crowed. "Lure 'em inside, shut 'em in, pile up the wood against the door, at the back, at the winder, at the weak places, and we got 'em, like rats-in-er-trap," he ended, running all his words together in his excitement. "We can do it, Miss Pym."

"This is stupid folly," snapped the marquis. "Take Miss

120

Grenier, Miss Pym, and make your way through the trees at the back until you come to a road and get her and her father to safety and let me have no more of your nonsense."

"But—"

"Do as you are told, woman!"

"How dare you!" said Sir George. "How dare you, sir? It strikes me as a brave and courageous idea and instead of standing there being rude to this excellent lady, why not show correct concern for Miss Grenier by taking her away yourself and relieving us of your singularly insulting and tedious presence."

"Oh, I stay with Miss Pym," said Yvonne.

"It is a bold but eminently sensible idea," said Monsieur Grenier quietly. "I, too, would like to see them caught."

The marquis felt baffled and humiliated. He wanted to protect Yvonne, to save her from danger, to play the hero he had longed to play while he had lain seething and helpless on the ground.

"Very well," he said suddenly, with a reluctant smile. "My apologies, Miss Pym. But do go outside and keep watch with Miss Grenier and leave us gentlemen to do the work."

Monsieur Grenier said he would start by making the dummies. Yvonne walked outside on Hannah's arm and took a deep breath of sweet clean air. "He came," said Hannah in a dazed way.

Yvonne gave her a hug. "He must be very fond of you."

Hannah's eyes clouded. "I fear he cannot have heard the scandal, and now I shall have to tell him. But let us sit down, Miss Grenier, and recover our strength for the ordeal ahead. If we sit down by the river, we will be able to hear the approach of any boat before they see us. We can hide behind that screen of bushes. Perhaps the marquis has the right of it and I should not be putting you at risk."

Yvonne tossed her head. "He is a bully, I think."

"Perhaps he is simply very deeply in love."

She sat down on the grass in the shade of the trees and

Yvonne sank gracefully down beside her. "I think our lord is a flirt," she said.

"Oh, no," said Hannah. "He flirts with such as the tiresome Dusty, for that is the polite and social thing to do. He does not flirt with you because his feelings are seriously engaged."

"You do not know the half of it. He kissed me."

"Well, I would suppose he would want to."

"Such a man must have kissed many ladies, but it was a first kiss for me. Besides, what honourable intentions can an English lord have towards a penniless French bourgeoise?"

"Love is a strange and painful thing," said Hannah sadly, for she was thinking of herself. Her initial heady elation at seeing Sir George was ebbing away, bit by bit. When this adventure was over, she would have to tell him what Benjamin had done, and he would grow cold and remote and that would be that.

Monsieur Grenier came out sometime later to say he needed some of their clothes to dress the dummies. Their pelisses, a petticoat each, and a bonnet would be enough. He kept watch on the river while they retreated farther into the trees to take off their petticoats. "I have pinned sacking over the window of the hut," he said when they emerged. "It must be so dark that all they get is an impression of bodies lying on the floor. Perhaps you can help me, Yvonne, and leave Miss Pym to keep watch." Yvonne and her father moved off, talking in rapid French. Hannah wondered what they were saying and whether Monsieur Grenier was asking about the marquis.

The men were working busily. They had a pile of tree trunks and saplings piled at the back of the hut in such a way that they could be moved quickly into place. "You may take a rest, sir," said the marquis to Sir George. "We cannot do anything else until the dummies are finished." Sir George had surrendered his coat and hat to Monsieur Grenier, as had Benjamin and the marquis. He reflected, as he walked down

122

to the river to join Hannah, that it was just as well the French gentleman hadn't thought it necessary to have his breeches as well.

He stopped before he came up to Hannah and stood for a few moments watching her. Her sandy hair was shiny and gleaming in the sun, a soft breeze ruffling the curls that Hannah had so assiduously created by sleeping with her hair in curl-papers.

He went forward and sank down onto the grass beside her. "So this is what you get up to on your travels," he said.

Hannah glanced sideways at him and blushed, because in his shirt-sleeves he seemed very masculine, approachable, no longer the well-tailored god of London days.

"While we wait, tell me all that has happened," he said.

And so Hannah told him all that she knew about Monsieur Petit, Yvonne and her father, and the marquis hardly believing as she spoke that Sir George was here with her, in the middle of an adventure.

"But you have not yet told me how you came to find me," said Hannah, once she had finished the tale of her adventures to date.

Hannah's strange eyes shone every colour of the rainbow as he told her of finding Mrs. Clarence while he was searching York for Miss Hannah Pym.

But the colour gradually went out of Hannah's eyes and she plucked nervously at a stem of grass.

"Why did you come to look for me?" she asked.

"Because I was bored," he said lightly, not wishing to distress her by telling her of the gossip about her that had been circulating society. "I could not wait for you to return to hear your latest adventure and so I decided to hunt you down. And now here I am in the thick of it."

Hannah turned a little pale, squared her shoulders, and said miserably, "You . . . you . . . would not have come had you known what Benjamin did, what Benjamin had said . . ."

"To be honest, that is one of the reasons I did come, Miss Pym. You see, I traced the gossip to its source . . ." Magnanimously, Sir George did not want to get Benjamin into trouble, as it was quite obvious that Miss Pym did not know her footman had written to him.

"I am so ashamed!" cried Hannah.

She made to jump to her feet but subsided as he laid a hand on her arm. "Stay. I did, I think, my best to scotch the rumour, and so here I am."

Tears welled up in Hannah's eyes. "I did not think you would want to see me again."

"My very dear friend, that is really why I came. I could not bear to think of your distress. We shall never refer to this matter again. I do not give up my friends because of tittle-tattle."

She should have been glad, relieved, but was conscious only of his hand on her arm and how breathless that contact was making her feel, of how she yearned for him while he smiled down on her with simple friendship in his eyes—and nothing else.

Hannah gave herself a mental shake. Her nerves were overset, she told herself severely, because of the excitements of the day. She prided herself on being a strong character, but no character, however strong, could feel other than weak and shaken after being rescued from a lingering death. Had she not prayed and hoped that the old friendship between them would be restored? Had she not told God that was all she wanted?

"Thank you," she said simply, ignoring the seventeen-year-old virgin inside who was crying, *Love me*. "I value your friendship."

The spry figure of Monsieur Grenier appeared outside the hut, calling to them.

He seemed amazingly recovered from his ordeal and appeared to be taking a childlike delight in the possible capture of his tormentors. But then, reflected Hannah, he was used to danger.

Monsieur Grenier led them to the hut and pointed proudly to the dummies on the floor. In the gloom of the hut they looked remarkably lifelike. Hannah bent down and peered closely. Her pelisse and petticoat had been stuffed with leaves. The "head" was made from scraps of paper and leaves; with the hat on top and the figure lying, as it were, face-down on the floor, it looked real enough.

The marquis, Benjamin, and Yvonne joined them. "Now," said the marquis, "I do not think we should loiter about here any longer. It is time to hide in the woods at the back. The fallen trees are piled round the side of the hut where we can easily roll them to block the door and also the window."

They followed him out of the gloom of the hut.

"We will now bolt the door at the front and wait," said the marquis. "When they are inside, Benjamin will help me with some other stout trees and branches and we will wedge the door closed tight so that even if they shoot the bolt away, they will not be able to escape. Then we will have them, as you so rightly said, Benjamin, like rats in a trap."

"What if one of them waits outside?" asked Yvonne.

"Then we will need to try to take him."

"What do we do now?" asked Hannah as they walked together into the shelter of the woods at the back of the hut.

"There is nothing we can do but wait," said the marquis. "Fortunately, the weather is warm," he added, looking at the ladies without their pelisses and the men without their coats. "I must apologize to you again, Miss Pym. What a sad, unadventurous fellow I must seem to you. But my fear was all for Miss Grenier, not for myself."

They chose a spot in a little glade. Benjamin was told to climb up one of the trees to where he could see the river.

The rest sat down on the grass. The marquis looked at Monsieur Grenier. "Now we have a moment's peace and quiet, can you tell me why they ransacked your room? We thought you had escaped them, for your toilet-case was gone."

"I kept it by me at work with a few personal belongings," said Monsieur Grenier. "Just in case I had to make a quick escape. But they came for me. They told me they had Yvonne. They were able to describe her and which stagecoach she had been travelling on. I did not think it a trick. I went meekly with them."

"But why search your papers?"

"A friend of mine escaped from France recently. He brought with him an interesting packet of papers. In it, there is proof that Petit was playing both sides of the fence before the Revolution, acting as a spy for the government for one group and spying against them for the other. He has been searching the papers of all us old collaborators, trying to get them back. He may have suspected that I have them."

"And do you?" asked Hannah.

"I have them in a pocket on the inside of my breeches. They did not search me, apart from making sure I was not armed."

"Why did you not send them back to France?" asked the marquis. "He would have been executed by his own tribunal."

"I waited too long. I was wondering who to send them to. Many on the tribunal were appointed by Petit and might conceal the evidence. What is your part in all this, milord?" asked Monsieur Grenier curiously.

Hannah listened eagerly, hoping he would say something about caring for Yvonne.

"I think I trust you all now enough to tell you the truth," said the marquis. "I was asked by the War Office to follow Monsieur Petit and find out what he was up to. That seemed a more interesting plan than picking him up right away. And so I met your daughter. I had to see you too, Monsieur

Grenier, to make sure that you really had turned against the Revolution. You worked for it once."

"Cannot you understand why?" pleaded Monsieur Grenier.

"Oh, yes, there are many in this country that are seduced by the idea of equality. It is not the ideals which are wrong but the uses of them. The bloodshed still goes on, I gather."

"From what I hear, yes." Monsieur Grenier gave a shudder. "Not the mass executions, not the crowds, but still enough to frighten and horrify."

"And will you continue to live in York?"

"With my daughter, yes. I can make a good living as a carpenter. So useful to have a second trade."

Sir George saw the disappointed look on Hannah's face and the way she looked from the marquis to Yvonne and thought with wry amusement that the travelling matchmaker could not for one moment give up her favourite pastime, even when she was sitting on the grass, minus hat, pelisse, and petticoat and waiting for the return of armed French spies.

Yvonne sat quietly, her hands folded, sunlight glinting in her hair and her long lashes shielding her eyes. When she had lain there, bound and gagged, she had been glad, yes, *glad*, that he had kissed her. That would be one memory to keep her warm as she mounted the scaffold with her father after some farce of a trial in Paris. She wished now that she had not supported Hannah in this folly of trying to trap Petit and Ashton. She wanted to get away and forget the marquis as soon as possible, begin a new life as a carpenter's daughter, and perhaps she would marry a carpenter's son, someone very worthy and honest and decent, who never would make her burn and sigh under the pressure of his lips.

There came a rustle in the leaves above her head and Benjamin dropped lightly out of the tree onto the grass. "There's four of 'em this time," he said, his clever, mobile cockney face almost ludicrous in its dismay.

"Damn," muttered the marquis. He looked Benjamin up and down. "Care for a mill?"

"Would I ever," said Benjamin with a grin.

"Stay here, the rest of you. Benjamin, come quickly. Let's hope they all go inside, but we will have to try to ambush perhaps two of them and get their weapons off them. Sir George, come with us as well. Shut and bolt the door as soon as you see the opportunity."

When they had gone, Hannah took Yvonne's hand. "We will creep to the edge of the woods, Yvonne. We may be able to be of help."

"Yes, Hannah," whispered Yvonne, neither woman bothering with the formality of surnames at such a time.

"I will come with you," said Monsieur Grenier softly.

They crouched down in some bushes and peered through. They could not see the marquis, Benjamin, or Sir George.

Mr. Ashton was first off the boat, a small cigar between his teeth and a gun at his hip. Behind him came Petit, but unarmed. Two burly-looking men followed them. "You can leave your weapons in the boat," Yvonne heard Monsieur Petit say in English. "Our little trussed pigeons will not be putting up any resistance."

"I say, Petit," drawled Ashton in English. "That Yvonne Grenier is a pretty piece. What say I have a bit of fun with her first?"

"When she is on board the ship, you may have all the fun you please," replied Monsieur Petit, and beside her in the bushes, Hannah felt Yvonne tremble, and whispered, "Courage!"

Ashton and Petit and their henchmen strolled up to the hut. Hannah waited, trying to control her suddenly rapid breathing.

Monsieur Petit and Mr. Ashton went into the hut and in

the next second, the marquis, Benjamin, and Sir George hurtled towards the two men who were waiting outside. While the marquis and Benjamin tackled the two men, Sir George slammed the door of the hut shut, bolted it, and lay against it, panting.

Hannah, Yvonne, and her father came out of the shelter of the bushes and watched anxiously.

Benjamin was grinning as he danced round one of the men. "Up with your dukes, monsoor," he crowed.

But the Marquis of Ware was not going to waste time playing the sportsman. He kicked his assailant in the stomach and when the man doubled over, brought him down with a vicious punch to the back of the neck.

Hannah gave an exclamation and ran headlong for the boat, where she seized one of the guns and ran back—just in time, for Benjamin's adversary had drawn a wicked-looking knife. Hannah rammed the gun into the Frenchman's neck and said, "Don't move." He did not understand what she said but he did understand what the pressure of the cold muzzle against his neck meant.

The marquis came up and took the gun from Hannah just as the Frenchman dropped his knife. Then the marquis brought the butt end of the gun down on his head and he sank unconscious on the grass. "The door," shouted the marquis, wheeling about as a gunshot sounded from inside the hut. "We forgot the door." He and Benjamin ran round to where the saplings and tree trunks were stacked and began to carry them round and pile them up against the door and then the window.

"Now help me tie these two here up," said the marquis. "What have we got?"

In the end, Hannah and Yvonne had to sacrifice the flounces from their gowns.

And just as they had finished and were standing beaming at each other, glad that the misery and fear were over, a posse of militia came crashing through the woods headed by John Hughes, Mrs. Clarence's ex-footman.

"Thank God it's all over," said Hannah, and the normally resolute Miss Pym buried her face in Sir George Clarence's shirt front and cried her eyes out.

8

She hugg'd the offender, and forgave the offence:
Sex to the last.

—John Dryden

That evening Hannah thought that they would all never be done with answering questions and giving statements to the magistrates. Ashton, Petit, and their two French henchmen were all in prison. The crew of the French boat, which had been lurking off Scarborough to take the Greniers to France, had all been arrested.

It was the marquis who, after a look at the strained whiteness of Yvonne's face, brought the interrogation to a close. He pointed out that the ladies were tired, and if necessary, they could be brought back on the following day.

As they stood outside the courtroom in York, the marquis said, "I feel sure none of us wants to return to Bradfield Park."

John Hughes spoke up. "Lucy will want to see Miss Pym and Sir George," he said. "With my boys being away, we have plenty of room for you all at the farm."

To Hannah's delight, everyone accepted the invitation,

even Sir George. She had been afraid that Sir George might opt to return to his room at the inn. Benjamin volunteered to go to Bradfield Park and collect their luggage after picking up Sir George's trunk from the Bull, and so they all set out in a large hired carriage for Rosewood Farm. Yvonne felt suddenly shy of all these English people. She felt she and her father had been forgotten. The marquis was making arrangements to call on Sir George at Thornton Hall when they returned to London, and Hannah was remarking that she was determined to have no more adventures. The only outing she wanted in the near future was a walk under the trees in Hyde Park. Sir George said gallantly that he would be delighted to escort her and Hannah's eyes gleamed with happiness.

But as they drew nearer to the farm, Hannah began to wonder how Mrs. Clarence would receive her. Mrs. Clarence had been her mistress. She might disapprove of an ex-servant's being on such familiar terms with her brother-in-law, although, Hannah reminded herself, Mrs. Clarence had run off with a footman, so had no reason to be high in the instep.

Benjamin had gone ahead of them with a trap to Bradfield Park and he arrived in the farmyard at the same time as they did.

For Hannah, the years rolled back as she saw the elegant figure of Mrs. Clarence standing on the steps of the farm. She felt suddenly shy and gauche, very much like the little scullery maid she had once been when the seventeen-year-old Mrs. Clarence had arrived to be mistress of Thornton Hall.

Sir George helped Hannah down from the carriage and Hannah sank into a low curtsy, but Mrs. Clarence ran forward and seized her hands, drew her to her feet, and gave her a fierce hug, and, as she had done in the past, found exactly the right words to say. "Why, Hannah Pym, what a great lady you have become. And how very stylish!"

Hannah was only thankful she was not wearing one of Mrs. Clarence's old gowns, for Mrs. Clarence had run away leaving all her clothes behind and Sir George had told Hannah after his brother's death she might have as many of the dresses, hats, and pelisses as she wanted to augment her meagre wardrobe.

She introduced Yvonne and her father and then the marquis. Mrs. Clarence looked sympathetically at Yvonne. "You poor little thing. How exhausted you must be! And how lost you must feel, with us all babbling away in English." Mrs. Clarence switched to fluent French. "So come with me. You are to share a bedchamber with Miss Pym. I do not think you should sit up talking. A good night's sleep is what you need."

The rest followed them in. The marquis was disappointed. He had hoped Yvonne would not go straight to bed, had hoped to study her for some signs of warmth and affection. The marquis knew he should now ask her father's permission before making any advance to her. "How frightful," sneered an arrogant voice in his head, "if you ask some French carpenter's daughter to marry you and she turns you down flat!" He immediately thought he was being pompous and ridiculous, and yet, in a way, could not bring himself to admit that he could not face the pain a rejection by her would give him.

He could only wonder at the resilience of Hannah Pym, who sat in the farm parlour with Benjamin behind her chair, talking and laughing, her eyes changing colour to suit her moods, looking as if nothing at all out of the way had happened to her during the day. Monsieur Grenier excused himself, saying he would like to speak to his daughter before she went to sleep.

The marquis watched him go. Would Yvonne tell him about that kiss?

Monsieur Grenier found his daughter climbing into bed. She smiled wearily at him and said softly, "It is hard to believe we are safe at last."

He sat down beside the bed and waited until she had settled herself against the pillows. "Tell me about this English marquis?" he asked.

Yvonne said in a neutral voice, "There is nothing much to tell. He came on the coach expressly to follow Monsieur Petit. He was . . . very kind. He paid for our accommodation on the road and in York. I . . . I need to repay him, Papa, for I accepted his generosity only as a loan."

"I had almost forgotten how beautiful you are, my child." Monsieur Grenier studied her face anxiously. "You have been moving in exalted company and I hope it has not turned your pretty head. These English aristocrats are very easy in their manner to all. They do not, however, marry below their rank."

"Of course not," said Yvonne wearily.

"You have been much in his company under unusual and frightening circumstances. Did he make any advances to you?"

"You forget, Papa, from the moment I left London, I was chaperoned by Miss Pym."

"Ah, yes. Miss Pym. Such a forceful lady, but with such a youthful heart. I admire her immensely. We shall find a little place to live in York, and then write to her, giving her our address."

"I would like that." Yvonne plucked at the coverlet. "It is doubtful, however, if we shall ever see any of them again."

He looked surprised. "But Mrs. Clarence is to help us find a place to live. And listen! She says we may stay here for a few days to recuperate. Like Miss Pym, she is an excellent lady. How did you come to meet her?"

In a soft, tired voice, Yvonne told him of Hannah's mistress who had run away with the footman. "I understand they are to be married next week."

"To find you under such a roof would normally shock me," said Monsieur Grenier, "but having met Mrs. Clarence, I cannot find her other than kind and beautiful. Now I will leave you to sleep." He rose and stood for a moment looking down at her. "You have been through much, Yvonne. I shall return to my old work at the carpentry shop. I am very good at it and they will be glad to have me back. Soon, I shall be able to give you a small dowry. There are many fine young men in the town among our compatriots."

He bent and kissed her cheek and then straightened up in surprise. "Tears, Yvonne? What is amiss?"

Yvonne turned her face away. "I am tired, Papa. Leave me now. All I need is a good night's sleep."

Monsieur Grenier made his way downstairs feeling uneasy. He hoped that Yvonne would settle down with him in York and find a husband. He stood for a moment on the threshold of the parlour, noticing for the first time how very handsome and virile a man the Marquis of Ware was. He was teasing Hannah about her adventures and his eyes glinted with mischief. What woman could resist such a man, thought Monsieur Grenier. He hoped the marquis had no plans to linger in York now that his work was finished. He remembered Yvonne's distress at the break-up of her engagement, a distress she had tried so hard to conceal from him. He would not like to see her hurt again.

And yet, as he moved into the room and sat down quietly, he could not help thinking that such a democratic gathering could never have existed in the France of his youth. Benjamin was being urged to take a chair and join the company and tell them his stories, which the footman gleefully did, at first in a rather strained, refined accent, and then lapsing into broad cockney, which Monsieur Grenier could barely understand.

At last everyone decided to retire for the night. Hannah went upstairs to the room she shared with Yvonne. Despite all her outward merriment, her sharp eyes had missed nothing. She had noticed the way Monsieur Grenier had studied the marquis on his return from saying good night to his daughter.

And then she noticed a familiar box on a table at her side of the bed. Wondering, she picked it up and opened it. On top was a note. "I took these back. I diddent think you wuld want to Lose them. Yr. Benjamin."

"Oh, you wonderful, silly boy," breathed Hannah, looking down at the presents Sir George had given her, along with that spoon from Gunter's and one worn kid glove.

For a brief moment, as she clutched her box of recovered treasures, she had a picture of an ancient Hannah Pym sitting in a cottage, turning over these mementoes and remembering when life had once been full of hope and colour. She gave herself a mental shake. Sir George was here, under Mrs. Clarence's roof. She would see him in the morning. Spinster and ex-servant that she was, she must enjoy his company while she had it, one moment at a time, and try not to think of the future.

Yvonne awoke at dawn. Beside her, Hannah slept tranquilly, her head a veritable forest of curl-papers. Yvonne tried to go back to sleep, but the birds were singing noisily and sunlight was shining through a chink in the curtains.

She decided to get up and go for a walk so as to compose her thoughts before she met the others again. She looked ruefully at her small stock of clothes and chose the least worn, a gown of green jaconet with only one flounce at the hem and a high neckline with a little ruff in the Elizabethan manner. It had been given her in lieu of payment by one of the ladies to whom she taught French. She pulled on a pair of half-boots, for the grass would be wet with the morning dew, and drew a large sage-green knitted woollen shawl about her shoulders.

It was Sunday morning and no one in the house was stirring. As she stepped out into the glory of the morning, she could hear the church bells of York sounding faintly across the fields. At least there was no tolling death bell. People in England were hanged on a Friday so that their souls might reach heaven by Sunday morning, the English, for all their occasional cruelty, believing that a merciful God would forgive even the worst murderer and allow him into Paradise.

She walked around the farmhouse and found a delightful garden at the back, knowing immediately it must have been planned by Mrs. Clarence. Red and white roses tumbled in breath-taking beauty from trellises set against the wall. At the foot of the garden ran a river, no doubt the same one which ran through Bradfield Park, thought Yvonne. It was bordered by willows, their leaves trailing in the slowly-moving glassiness of the water, which mirrored the puffy white clouds sailing high above in a sky of pure cerulean. The sun was already warm on her head. There was a rustic seat by the river. She sat down on it and watched the moving water and leaves, in that moment happy and content.

Yvonne heard a soft step on the grass behind her and reluctantly turned her head, shading her eyes against the sun, to see who it was.

The Marquis of Ware stood there. He was impeccably dressed in ruffled shirt, blue coat, breeches, and boots, his hat set at a rakish angle on his head. She felt a sudden pang and asked quickly, "Are you leaving us?"

"Only to go to York," he said, sitting down beside her. "I will see if I can give them all the facts they want so that they will leave all of you to enjoy your day in peace. Did you sleep well?"

"Yes, I thank you."

"You are a symphony in green," he said, his voice light and mocking. "Green grass, green trees, and a green girl."

"I did not expect company, milord," said Yvonne stiffly.

"So what are your plans for the future now that you are reunited with your father?"

"We talked about it last night. He will return to his job at the carpentry shop. Mrs. Clarence says we may stay with her until we find somewhere to live. The room above the greengrocer's is not suitable for both of us."

"And what will you do?"

"I will find employ as a French teacher and seamstress and work at building up a dowry. Then Papa will no doubt find me a suitable husband among the ranks of our own countrymen. And what of you, milord?"

"Return to my house in the country, after a few weeks in London, to my estates."

"But not by stage-coach?"

"No, my chuck, definitely not by stage-coach. I will leave that mode of travel to such as Miss Pym."

"Sir George does not appear to have taken offence over the scandal," said Yvonne.

"I suppose it would be so absolutely ridiculous if he did," commented the marquis. "I mean, *Miss Pym* the mistress of anybody or, for that matter, anybody's wife!"

"How stupid you are," said Yvonne, reverting to French in her anger. "How stupid and unseeing."

"You amaze me," he retorted in the same language. "I believe you have romantical notions of making a match of it with Miss Pym and Sir George—a practical Frenchwoman such as yourself who plans to stitch and sew and teach dull ladies French, all in order to buy herself a husband. You had better make sure your dowry is up to his expectations or he may run off like your last love."

He then sat there stunned at his own cruelty, for her face flamed, tears started to her eyes, and she jumped to her feet.

He got up quickly as well and caught her arm as she would have run from him, crying, "Forgive me, Miss Grenier . . . Yvonne . . . please stay."

She tried to pull free and all his ease of manner deserted him and the Marquis of Ware blurted out like a schoolboy, "I want you for myself."

She stood very still, the sun in her hair. She heard the chuckle of the river and the song of the birds.

"You want me as your chère-amie," she said flatly.

"No. I should have spoken to your father first. But I looked out of my window and saw you in the garden and . . . and . . . oh, Yvonne Grenier, I want you as my wife."

He released her arm. He took off his hat and stood

humbly before her, watching the rapid changing emotions fleeting across her expressive face.

Her eyes began to glow and she said softly, "But you cannot marry a carpenter's daughter."

"Your father will no longer have to work."

She peeped up at him shyly. "Are . . . are you sure? Are you really sure you want to marry me?"

He tossed away his hat. He swept her into his arms and bent his mouth to hers, lost as he had been before in the taste of her lips and the feel of her pliant body against his own. The world began to spin around them, slowly turning in whirling darkness with themselves at its axis, as he kissed her lips, her nose, her cheeks, and her lips again, trying to rein his mounting passion, but all the time feeling it fuelled by the passion in the slight body he held so tightly against him.

Above them, Hannah Pym leaned her elbows on the sun-warmed windowsill and watched them with interest. Then she ducked back inside and went downstairs to make sure no one wandered out to disturb the passionate lovers in the garden.

Benjamin came into the parlour while Hannah was sitting at an open window, enjoying the morning air. She looked up. "Thank you for my box, Benjamin," she said. "You are the best of servants."

"Thought you might want them back after a bit," mumbled Benjamin. He opened his mouth to tell her he had written to Sir George and then decided against it. Sir George had obviously said nothing about it. He wondered what was going on between that unlikely pair—Hannah Pym and Sir George Clarence. They had faced possible death together, Sir George had come to her rescue, and yet that had not seemed to spark any loverlike light in the retired diplomat's eye. It was not that Benjamin particularly wanted Hannah to marry. It was just that he dreaded that future she had planned of life in a small cottage. If she were married to Sir George, then she would live in London, and Benjamin really could not envisage living anywhere else. And over and above that, Miss Pym wanted Sir George, and Benjamin saw no reason why she shouldn't have him.

Monsieur Grenier came into the room, bowed before Hannah, and then raised her hand to his lips. "I have not yet had time, Miss Pym," he said, "to thank you for taking care of my daughter. You are a courageous and gallant lady."

Hannah's sallow face flushed with pleasure. "What a beautiful morning," exclaimed Monsieur Grenier. "Would you care to promenade with me, Miss Pym?"

Hannah thought very quickly. She did not want the couple in the garden disturbed. On the other hand, what if the marquis had not proposed marriage? And they had had time enough.

She made up her mind. "Yes, I should like that very much, Monsieur Grenier. Benjamin, you may remain here."

Benjamin stood at the window and watched the couple cross the farmyard to the gate leading to the garden. Hannah stumbled on a pebble and Monsieur Grenier put an arm around her waist to steady her.

Now, thought Benjamin, there's a thing. They look quite a pair. I wonder if that old fossil could be made jealous—the old fossil being Sir George.

The couple had just entered the garden when Monsieur Grenier stopped short and stared appalled at the tableau in front of him. He daughter was being ferociously kissed by the Marquis of Ware and appeared to be enjoying every minute of it.

"No, no, no!" he cried out, and the couple broke apart.

Hannah put a hand on Monsieur Grenier's arm and said in a quiet voice, "I think my lord has something to ask you."

The marquis took Yvonne's hand in his and said simply, "I wish to marry your daughter, sir. I hope we have your blessing."

"Marry!" Monsieur Grenier looked at them in a bewildered way. His plans for his daughter had been made. They would find a little house and work hard and then one day Yvonne would marry a young Frenchman. But a marquis!

"I do not think, milord, that you have given the matter enough thought," he said. "You have the grand house, non? And many servants? Such grandeur. My daughter is used to a humbler mode of life."

"I am not marrying your daughter to gain a house-keeper, sir," said the marquis. "I am going to marry her because I love her and cannot live without her."

Hannah felt a pang of sadness. No man would ever say such glorious words to her.

"Monsieur Grenier and I should go indoors, where we can discuss this matter in private. Miss Pym, will you keep Miss Grenier company?"

He and the Frenchman walked off, already deep in discussion by the time they had reached the garden gate.

"What have they to discuss?" demanded Yvonne impatiently. "I love him, he loves me, and that is all that matters."

"I think your papa will want to know about marriage settlements," said Hannah. "Let us sit down and admire the river. Yes, marriage settlements are very important."

"He is keeping Lord Ware back from going to York," fretted Yvonne. "He was going to go into the town and answer all the necessary questions on behalf of the rest of us, so that we should not be plagued further."

"I am sure your father will not keep him long," said Hannah.

"But what if Papa sets his face against the marriage? He might persuade Ware that it would not work, our back-grounds being so very different."

"You are worrying and worrying to no good avail," said Hannah bracingly. Then her boundless curiosity made her ask, "Do you call him Ware when you are . . . er . . ."

Yvonne blushed and laughed. "I do not even know his Christian name."

"You should read the social columns more often," said Hannah. "It is Rupert."

"Rupert," echoed Yvonne dreamily.

They sat in companionable silence for about half an hour until Yvonne began to feel uneasy again. She was just beginning to say, "I think they have had time enough," when the marquis and her father came back into the garden.

Yvonne ran to meet the marquis and stood beside him, looking at her father with wide anxious eyes. He raised his hands. "You both have my blessing."

Hannah warmly congratulated both. Then Mrs. Clarence came into the garden to be told the glad news. "Weddings are in the air," she said merrily. "Miss Pym, dear Hannah, I would be most honoured if you would be my bridesmaid at my wedding. Sir George is to give me away."

Hannah agreed while her heart raced. She would be able to stay with Sir George for another whole week. She felt so very happy all at once, she thought she would burst.

"Now I must go to York," said the marquis. "I will not be very long."

"And Miss Pym and I will continue our walk," said Monsieur Grenier. He bowed and held out his arm. Hannah glanced up at the windows of the farm and saw Sir George looking down at the group in the garden. Instead of waving to him, something prompted her to give Monsieur Grenier a flirtatious look as she took his arm.

Yvonne was saying a prolonged goodbye to the marquis in the farmyard as Mrs. Clarence entered the house. Benjamin was standing moodily in the shadowy hall. "If you are looking for Miss Pym, she is out walking with Monsieur Grenier," said Mrs. Clarence.

"May I ask your advice, modom?" said Benjamin stiffly.

"Of course. Follow me." Mrs. Clarence led the way to a little morning-room at the back of the hall. It overlooked the garden. There was no sign of either Hannah or Monsieur Grenier.

Mrs. Clarence sat down in an easy chair and Benjamin stood before her. "You may take a chair, Benjamin," said Mrs. Clarence. "If I may say so, the Hannah Pym I knew would not have allowed any servant the licence she gives you. You are an odd sort of footman."

"Would die for 'er," said Benjamin in a choked voice.

"Your loyalty does you credit, young man. Now, how can I help you?"

Benjamin leaned forward eagerly. "It's like this. Miss Pym is sweet on Sir George an' it would be a great match."

"Sir George," said Mrs. Clarence cautiously, "is very fond of Miss Pym. Anyone can see that. But someone like my brother-in-law who has remained a bachelor for so long is usually not romantically inclined."

"But worth a try," said Benjamin eagerly. "Surely worth a try."

She echoed Benjamin's earlier thoughts. "George has already been in the most romantical situation possible with Miss Pym. He saved her life and shared her adventure. I do not know what else can be done."

"Jealousy," said Benjamin. "That might get his mind on the right track."

"Are you proposing to woo your mistress in an attempt to make Sir George jealous?"

"No!" Benjamin looked horrified. "Not me. That Monsoor Grenier might do the trick."

"Aha!"

"Exactly."

"But subtlety, Benjamin, is what is required. One cannot be too obvious. You must leave matters to me. Now, no one has had any breakfast with all this talk of weddings. Do you know that Lord Ware and Miss Grenier are to marry?"

"No, modom," said the footman, "but that don't surprise me. Miss Pym probably arranged it. She's only to look at a couple and they start thinkin' of gettin' wed."

"Go and fetch Sir George and tell him to come to the

dining-room for breakfast. We will save something for Miss Pym and her gallant if they are not back soon."

Over a hearty breakfast, Sir George and John Hughes heard all about Yvonne's forthcoming marriage, and Yvonne sat glowing with happiness.

"But where is our travelling matchmaker?" asked Sir George. "Miss Pym dearly loves to arrange weddings."

"Miss Pym knows all about it," said Mrs. Clarence. "She is out walking with Monsieur Grenier. They should not be long. Neither of them has breakfasted."

But two more hours passed and there was no sign of Hannah Pym. Sir George was beginning to become anxious, wondering if there might be more dangerous Frenchmen lurking about. At last he seized his hat and said he would go out to look for her.

Hannah and Monsieur Grenier had left the garden a long time ago and wandered off into the countryside, Hannah determined to stay away as long as possible to show Sir George that another man found her company welcome. For his part, Monsieur Grenier felt he had not had such a sympathetic audience in a long time. With all the worries and terrors of France, he had hardly had time even to mourn his wife's death. They came to a fallen log on top of a rise overlooking a field of corn, which rose and fell under a summer breeze in golden waves like the sea.

Hannah encouraged him to talk on, wondering all the while whether her absence from the farmhouse had been remarked on by Sir George. To do her justice, she did realize that the Frenchman needed to talk and listened sympathetically and even completely forgot about Sir George when Monsieur Grenier began to cry over the death of his wife and then over the murder of his friends who had been dragged to the guillotine. When he had recovered, she asked him what he would do once Yvonne was married and he replied that he had not had time to think about it. The marquis had told him that he need never work again, but he was used to working and dreaded being idle. Perhaps he might study for the English bar.

His stomach gave an ungentlemanly rumble and so Hannah reminded him that neither of them had had anything to eat that day and they strolled back amicably to the farmhouse. Monsieur Grenier began to feel happier and happier as they neared the farm. He had talked away all his pain and fears and worries. His future now looked as golden as the day. His daughter was to marry a man she loved. They were safe at last. He did not see Sir George bearing down on them. He turned impulsively to Hannah and cried, "You have taken so much of my pain away. You are a wonderful lady! A great lady!" And he seized the astonished Hannah and kissed her resoundingly on both cheeks. Hannah blushed and laughed and then saw Sir George standing looking at them.

Sir George's first incoherent thought was that Hannah had no right to be kissed by anyone while she was wearing the scarf he had given her. The second was that she should not be ambling around the country with a foreigner without even a hat on her head, her thick, sandy, shiny curls making her look appealingly youthful.

But his diplomat's eyes quickly veiled his thoughts and he greeted them politely and reminded them they had not breakfasted. He accompanied them back to the inn, thinking crossly that Monsieur Grenier, who had taken Hannah's arm, did not need to assume such a, well, proprietorial air.

"I do believe," said Mrs. Clarence over her shoulder to Benjamin, as she watched the trio arrive, "that our Miss Pym is doing very well all by herself."

Sir George said mildly enough that the air was making him surprisingly hungry again and he thought he would join Miss Pym and Monsieur Grenier at the breakfast table.

When they had finished eating, Sir George asked Hannah to show him the garden. But they found an odd constraint had fallen between them. Hannah could not talk on in her usual easy way with him, and felt tongue-tied and gauche.

She could not seem to shake this odd constraint off, and because of it, during the rest of that day and the following ones, gravitated more and more to Monsieur Grenier's undemanding company.

To Sir George's great irritation, Mrs. Clarence appeared to be encouraging Miss Pym to spend more time with Monsieur Grenier than Sir George considered decent. He feared that the marquis would decide to convey Yvonne and her father to London and so he would be encumbered with their company when he himself escorted Miss Pym south, and was relieved when he learned that the marquis had obtained a special licence and planned to wed Yvonne in York a week after Mrs. Clarence. His relief was short-lived. Hannah was to be bridesmaid again at Yvonne's wedding to the marquis.

The marquis had pressed for a quick wedding, for his passion for Yvonne was growing with every kiss. Monsieur Grenier was elated with happiness at being safe at last and at the sight of his daughter's joy, but Sir George decided bitterly that the Frenchman's elation was caused by love for Hannah Pym.

The day of Mrs. Clarence's wedding arrived. It was to take place in the farmhouse, which had been decorated with garlands for the occasion. No neighbours had been invited, all believing that she and John Hughes were already married. Mrs. Clarence had explained she would tell her sons sometime in the future when she thought the moment was right. Even the servants and farm-hands had been sent away for the day.

Hannah had been gowned in shot silk by Mrs. Clarence for her role of bridesmaid, and Sir George reflected she had never looked better. When the simple service was over and they sat down to the wedding breakfast, served to them, in the absence of other servants, by Benjamin, Sir George found that Hannah had been placed next to him while Monsieur Grenier was on her other side. Hannah meticulously conversed to Sir George and Monsieur Grenier, giving each an equal share of her time, but Sir George could not help hearing how easily she chatted to the Frenchman while all her conversation with him was awkward and stilted. He felt quite old and dried up. In the past week, he felt he had aged daily while Hannah appeared to have grown younger.

He suddenly rose to his feet and announced to the surprised assembly that he had the headache and needed some fresh air. When the door had closed behind him, Monsieur Grenier said quietly to Hannah, "My dear friend, I feel you have made that gentleman miserable enough. Why do you not go after him?"

Hannah looked at the little Frenchman and coloured guiltily. How did he know? How had he guessed? She opened her mouth to protest she did not know what he meant, thought better of it, and quietly left the room.

She stood a few moments later at the entrance to the garden. Sir George was sitting on the rustic bench by the river. He was hatless and his hair gleamed like silver in the sun. The air was sultry and warm and, to the west, great black clouds were piling up against the sky as if climbing on top of each other. From the distance came a menacing growl of thunder.

Hannah walked forward and sat down beside him. "Is your head better?" she asked gently.

"Yes, I thank you." Sir George looked at the silver buckles on his shoes as if they were the most fascinating things he had ever seen.

"Perhaps I can fetch you something from the house? A posset, perhaps?"

"No, no. It would be better to leave me alone, Miss Pym."

"Very well." She rose sadly to her feet.

"I mean, no, sit down, I mean, well, I did not mean to sound so harsh . . . I mean . . . I am a trifle overset." He waved a hand at the sky. "Storms affect my nerves, I think."

Thunder growled and rumbled, nearer now, and a sharp puff of warm wind ruffled the surface of the river.

Hannah sat down primly, bottom on the very edge of the seat, back ramrod-straight. Her violet silk gown was shot with gold and glinted and shone oddly in the now gloomy green light of the garden under the fast-approaching storm.

"You seem to . . . to . . . be very friendly with Monsieur Grenier," said Sir George.

"He is a charming and sympathetic gentleman," said Hannah. "He likes talking to me, I think."

He turned to her. "Miss Pym, as your friend and advisor, I must take it upon myself to counsel you to be cautious. Marriage to a foreigner can be . . . well . . . cannot be a good thing for an Englishwoman."

"English royalty marry foreigners the whole time," said Hannah flatly.

"What the bleedin't 'ell's goin' on?" shouted Benjamin, jumping up and down in frustration behind the backs of the watchers now crowded around an upstairs window of the farmhouse that overlooked the garden.

"Nothing yet," said the new Mrs. Hughes over her shoulder. "And if they don't come in soon, they are both going to get very wet."

"You know what I mean, Miss Pym," Sir George was saying. "I am concerned for your welfare, your future."

"Do not worry, Sir George," said Hannah, "I am surely old enough to look after myself."

"Oh, indeed, madam? And what would have become of you in that hut if I had not come along? You lead an irresponsible life. Traipsing up and down the length and breadth of England with that popinjay of a footman."

"Now, sir, you go too far. Benjamin is a brave and loyal servant and I will not have a word said against him. He has volunteered to settle down with me in some poky cottage in the country, and that is a great sacrifice for such a clever and fun-loving fellow."

Sir George looked at her, appalled. "I was wrong. It is not Monsieur Grenier you plan to marry but your own footman."

"What are you about?" raged Hannah. "What has come over you? You know you are talking fustian. What on earth is the matter with you?"

"I'm in love with you, demme," roared Sir George, "and I don't know what to do."

Hannah looked at him in sheer amazement. "Well, you could try marrying me, for a start."

"Miss Pym . . . Hannah . . . do you mean you would accept me?"

A great crack of thunder sounded overhead. "Sir George," said Hannah patiently, "I think I have been in love with you since that morning when you found me standing by the window of Thornton Hall, watching the stage-coach go past."

He drew her into his arms and bent his head and kissed her gently on the mouth. Another crack of thunder drowned out the cheer from the farmhouse window behind them. It was pleasant kissing Hannah Pym, thought Sir George dreamily, settling her more comfortably in his arms, warm and sweet like the air around them and lit with flashes of lightning like the sky above.

The rain began to pour down on the kissing couple, at first in great warm drops and then in a steady flood.

"Come away immediately," said Monsieur Grenier sternly, drawing his giggling daughter away from the window.

"Quite a goer is our Miss Pym," said the marquis in wonder, "and who would have thought an old stick like Sir George would have all that fire locked up in his diplomatic bosom?"

The watchers tactfully withdrew from the window. Benjamin lingered and took a peek outside and then executed a couple of cartwheels down the corridor before following the rest of them downstairs.

Two months had passed by the time Hannah, now Lady George Clarence, returned to Thornton Hall after a quiet wedding in a London church. It was to be the first night of her marriage. Benjamin had stayed behind at South Audley Street to pack everything up.

Hannah undressed with quick agitated fingers, feeling it all very strange to find herself back at Thornton Hall and mistress of it now.

She felt very nervous and frightened of the night to come but had been unable to bring herself to say anything to Sir George. She could not explain that she felt like a virginal seventeen-year-old. She put on the delicate lace-and-cambric night-gown which had been a present from Mrs. Clarence, now Mrs. Hughes, and climbed into bed and lay straight and flat like a patient on a surgeon's table. She was cold with nerves. Her hands were cold and clammy and her feet were like ice.

Sir George came in and went about the great bedchamber blowing out the candles. He climbed into bed and gathered Hannah in his arms and all fear and coldness fled at his touch.

She awoke automatically early in the morning and climbed from the bed. She drew back the curtains and opened the shutters and stood at the window.

Along the Kensington road came the Exeter mail, the horses steaming and pounding the flat road, the roof passengers hanging on to their hats.

"Come back to bed, Hannah," came Sir George's amused voice. "You're home now. Your journeys are over."

She turned and smiled shyly at him and went back into bed and into his arms as the coaches continued to move out from London, along the dusty roads of England, to other loves, other meetings, and other happy endings.

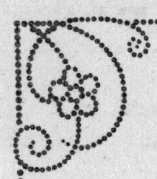

MARION CHESNEY'S
The School for Manners

Join Amy and Effy Tribble as they seek to bring to heel the most *irrepressible* young women in Regency London!

REFINING FELICITY #1
_____ 91585-3 $3.50 U.S./91586-1 $4.50 CAN.

PERFECTING FIONA #2
_____ 92059-8 $3.50 U.S./92060-1 $4.50 CAN.

ENLIGHTENING DELILAH #3
_____ 92157-8 $3.50 U.S./$4.50 CAN.

FINESSING CLARISSA #4
_____ 92283-3 $3.95 U.S./$4.95 CAN.

ANIMATING MARIA #5
_____ 92343-0 $3.95 U.S./$4.95 CAN.

MARRYING HARRIET #6
_____ 92420-8 $3.95 U.S./$4.95 CAN.